MODERN HINDI SHORT STORIES

INTRODUCTION BY **RAJSHREE BOSE**

MODERN HINDI SHORT STORIES

FOREWORD BY

BHISHAM SAHNI

Srishti
PUBLISHERS & DISTRIBUTORS

Srishti Publishers & Distributors
A unit of AJR Publishing LLP
212A, Peacock Lane
Shahpur Jat, New Delhi – 110 049
editorial@srishtipublishers.com

First published by
Srishti Publishers & Distributors in 2020

10 9 8 7 6 5 4 3 2 1

Contents

Foreword

I do not know how it feels, reading Hindi short stories rendered into the English language. Much of the linguistic flavour is bound to get lost; also much of the typical idioms rich in association, the turn of phrase, colloquialism, expressions with their nuances, etc. Hindi today is being written, not only by those who live in the so-called 'Hindi belt' (by itself a very large area with many dialects), but also by a large number of writers whose mother-tongue is not Hindi and who hail from practically every state and region of India. Thus, Hindi today takes on the colour of the local idiom, the traditional sayings of different localities and proverbs etc., and consequently the Hindi short story today reflects the spoken idiom and life and customs and social relationships of many areas in the country, the rich diversity of the cultural milieu of different regions and areas. This rich diversity of linguistic expression puts considerable strain on the translator who is called upon to transmit both the sense, and the flavour through the English language.

The language used has a rich texture, but thematically the Hindi short story has not opened out to many vistas of experience. There has been a lot of experimentation with form, there have also been different trends at work, but mostly, the stories have moved within the sphere of urban middle-class life. This may sound strange. But it has had its own peculiar reasons. After the attainment of Independence, many writers gravitated to metropolitan cities like Delhi, Calcutta, Bombay, etc. These centres afforded better opportunities for their work: the radio, the television, numerous journals, and publishing houses offered them better scope for pursuing their literary ambitions. (There are very few Hindi writers who can live by their pen.) Soon enough, they found that their area of experience was getting more and more confined to city life and largely to the life of the middle-class. These writers had brought with them memories and influences of their small-town or rural life where they had spent their younger days. Sometimes, either nostalgia or a sense of social concern prompted them to write stories based on their earlier experiences and observations. Sometimes the domestic servant, the labourer on construction site, the coolie, the rickshaw-puller or even the lumpens in city life drew their attention and they wrote stories about them. But generally, the range of experience remained rather limited. Of late, some very penetrating stories have been appearing, giving us close glimpses of the life of the landless poor, or of the migrant field labourer! Also, stories relating to the burning issues of social life, like the communal question, position of women in society, etc., a trend which is becoming quite dominant in Hindi writing. Yet, by and large, the stories deal with the middle and lower middle-class life.

The Hindi writer still does not feel very comfortable with the urban rich or with the industrial houses or the vast underworld that is fast developing in the big cities. Stories have been written about them, but they lack the ring of authenticity. Man-woman relationship has been the age-long theme of stories and it continues to be so today also, despite the powerful trend focussed on the struggle for survival and for social justice. Over the years, there has been a lot of experimentation and search for form in the Hindi short story. There is a saying among Hindi writers that, after every ten years, a new trend appears in Hindi short story writing, accompanied by a lot of fan-fare and publicity. Researchers have even pin-pointed dates and months and years. It was thus that trends like the *'nai kahani'* (the new story), the *'sachetan kahani'* (the conscious story), the *'a-kahani'* (the non-story), the *'samanantar kahani'* (the parallel story), etc., appeared from time to time. These trends may not necessarily denote any real change in the form and content of the story or any significant shift in the direction of its development, but they do reflect lively interest and involvement with the genre, particularly in each case of the younger set of writers.

In the tone and temper of the Hindi short story, however, there has been a marked change. There is less of the old sentimentality, less of the old romantic incredibility; the temptation to moralise is also held under check. The story has certainly moved closer to life. It has become somewhat more earnest and serious, sometimes even sombre. The old playfulness and even flippancy of the earlier humorous writing has given place to sharp, at times bitter, satire. A trend of angry protest, which had appeared soon after Independence, and which, in its earlier phases, went by the name of 'disillusionment', has continued unabated. There is much greater involvement with social issues now.

There is another trend, rather introspective in nature, and deeply influenced by the Western literature of alienation, which has made considerable contribution to the Hindi short story writing. The stories may not directly reflect the Indian reality and may largely tend to be abstract and introvert, yet their depiction of the working of the human mind, the subtle nuances in the use of words, the lyricism, the creation of mood and atmosphere are noteworthy.

The Hindi short story moves largely in the midst of lower middle-class life and characters. This class offers the greatest variety in terms of character. The lower middle-class man can be a naive, a simpleton, but he is at times best equipped with passion and idealistic fervour. The Hindi writer shows a better understanding of characters from this class than from any other class, largely because the writers themselves, by and large, come from this class.

The sensibility of the Hindi writer is reacting more and more sharply to the throb of life around him, to the anxiety and apprehension that fill the atmosphere. He wants to penetrate deeper into life and identify the elements that cause this anxiety and apprehension. He may not be very discerning, he may at times apply simplistic criteria, but his keen sense of concern is very visible, and is increasingly becoming more intense.

Such, briefly, is the situation concerning Hindi short story writing. Despite numerous handicaps and weaknesses, the

Hindi short story still remains the most eloquent and dynamic genre in Hindi writing today.

Jai Ratan, a veteran in the field of translation, has presented in this collection a wide spectrum of what is being written in the sphere of the Hindi short story. He is an adept in the three north Indian languages – Hindi, Urdu and Punjabi – besides the English language into which he has been translating works of fiction from all these three languages for well over three decades. One can build a small library with his translations. Those of us who know the situation as it prevails in our country in respect of translation-work and the publication of translations will appreciate the truly Herculean task that he has pursued all these years. It has largely been a labour of love. The reward in terms of material gain is a mere pittance contrasted with the effort put in. For him, to have made this selection could not have been easy. There are three generations of short story writers writing these days, and, judging from their sheer number, it must have been a formidable task. To sift and choose, and to see that an authentic collection is presented reflecting the different trends, styles, and attitudes to life from the big pile of all kinds of stories, could not have been easy. The list of authors, and their stories presented, should convince the reader that the compiler and translator has done his best to make this volume as representative as possible.

BHISHAM SAHNI

Introduction

Modern Hindi Short Stories is a collection of some invaluable short tales. A collection of some of the choicest inspirational Hindi stories which are sure to leave you with some important life lessons. Every story is unique in itself, and every story hides in its folds a special message for the reader.

This book mainly focuses on the struggles of life and livelihood. This book also focuses on the complexities women are subjected to in our society, and their circumstances that drive them into becoming what they are. In more ways than one, this is a very sensitive book. Along with all this, the stories in this book also reflect the life in rural environment as against the urban setting – an obstacle that many had to face with the drastic changes post-Independence.

For instance, the story by Phanishwarnath Renu draws our attention to the incivilities of the rural life on the one hand, and also on the other hand introduces us to the reality of the relationship between the rural and urban lifestyle. His story is a perfect example of human compassion. Similarly, storyteller

Rajendra Yadav has written the story in simple yet captivating words, which urge the reader to finish the suspenseful story from the beginning till the end in one go.

Nirmal Varma has brought together various elements of newness into his story to make it a melting pot of emotions, and yet an awe-inspiring experience in itself. His story is greatly reflective of the diverse dimensions of a sensitive intellectual's excitement towards life, his dilemma, and the loneliness – all in a very symbolic way.

That is why this book is a treasure of many specials. Each character in these stories has been crafted with utmost attention, keeping in mind the little nuances. This book is an attempt to put together stories that can join the reader with his/ her life values in today's society and social circumstances.

Since these are all short stories and short reads, I entreat you to look at them as a window to finding positivity in everyday life, no matter what hurdle life throws at you. With this, I wish all the readers luck and lots of love.

RAJSHREE BOSE

1

The Fragrance of a Primitive Night

Phanishwarnath Renu

Phanishwarnath Renu was born in 1921 in a village in Bihar and participated in the Quit India movement of 1942. He came into the limelight in 1954 with his first novel *Maila Anchal,* which broke new ground in Hindi fiction. His next novel *Parti Parikatha* appeared in 1957, and a collection of short stories in 1959. One of his stories was made into a film. His novel *Maila Anchal* and many of his stories have been translated into English and other languages. He breathed his last in 1977.

No, he wouldn't be able to sleep – Karma knew it. He never felt at home in a newly-constructed brick house- the acrid smell of lime and fresh varnish would cause a pain to flare up behind his ear, a pain the size of a four-anna coin. It would keep throbbing all the lime. The old railway stations on the old rail route – that was where he liked to be. Ancient, no doubt. But he could sleep soundly under their roof. Oh, hell! His nostrils had again started tingling.

Karma sneezed, its sound exploding in the new house.

The Babu was lying on a camp cot.

"Karma, are you still awake?" he asked turning on his side.

"I won't be able to sleep here," Karma said, wiping his nose with his *gamchha.* "I knew it Babu."

"Nor can I." The Babu lighted a cigarette. "It's always like that with me. I miss my sleep under a new roof, the first night in any case."

Karma wanted to ask the Babu if he was also tormented by the smell of damp lime in a new house. Did his jaw also throb with pain behind the ear? But the Babu had started singing under his breath.

Karma saw a pariah dog coming from the direction of the signal cabin. It slopped near the verandah. Karma watched it warily, trying to anticipate its next move. Raising its snout towards the Babu's cot, the dog sniffed in the air and then advanced. Karma knew the dog. It was a shoe-stealer. *Sala!* Did it really mean business? The dog turned towards Karma, again sniffed in the air and then trotted off in the direction of the passengers' waiting hall.

"Boy, what's your name?" the Babu asked him. "Karma, Karam Chand or Karmu?"

The question pleased Karma. It was the first time in the seven days they had been together that the Babu had shed his reserve.

"Babu, they call me Karma. That's my real name. But you know there are as many tongues as there are mouths. Netai Babu called me Karma, Ghosh Babu called me Krima while Singhji always addressed me as Kama. And as for Asghar Babu, he always called me by the name of Karm. When in a gay mood, he would say, 'Oh, my Karm, the living, walking symbol of my misdeeds!' But what's in a name, Babu? I am what I am."

"Where's your home? In the Santhal Parganas? In the district of Ranchi? Hazaribagh?"

Karma hesitated for a moment. When faced with such a question, he put on an all-knowing look, as though he belonged to the whole world. "God is my *mai-bap*," he wanted to say. "And where my body happens to be, that's where my home is." But he could not give such impish replies to the Babu.

A clever Babu indeed! Hadn't he guessed from Karma's name and the structure of his forehead where he hailed from? It was after a long time that he had come across a man as wise and clever as Gopal Babu.

"Babu," Karma said, "Gopal Babu also said the same. In fact it was Gopal Babu who gave me this name."

Gopal Babu's name triggered off memories that had till now remained dormant in his mind. "Gopal Babu said I was discovered in a wooden crate on a goods train coming from Assam. Without any tag, without any label. Unclaimed property!"

Lo and behold, the Babu had dozed off! Tch! He had to stop midway, leaving Gopal Babu's story incomplete. Oh, how he snored!

The pariah dog again appeared on the scene. It was the month of Kartik.

The wretch must have gone after a bitch, the way it was panting. "So you want to sleep here?" Oh, how it smelled! "Tut, tut! Be gone!"

"Then what happened to your Gopal Babu?" The Babu had suddenly come awake.

Karma was still looking at the dog. It had climbed down the verandah, stopped, looked back, growled and then barking in a low key had disappeared into the ladies' waiting room.

"Babu, have you gone to sleep again?"

Yes, the Babu had again dozed off, snoring like a typical Babu. When the pointsman snored, he sounded as if he was sawing wood, and Gopal Babu as if he was playing on a bagpipe. He snored in a perfectly well-modulated key.

The tinkle of the telegraph office, the bell of the railway station, the guard's whistle, the engine's bugle and the river-boat's hoot. And now the Babu's snoring ... a medley of whistling sounds.

Karma tried hard but he could not extricate himself from the railway track. He struggled, writhed, cried, but his body remained glued to the track. The engine thundered past, tearing apart his legs and neck. He hurriedly collected his trunkless legs. Thank God, they were not his legs but Anthony Guard Saheb's pair of gumboots, But what had happened to his head? The dog was nibbling at his nose and ears.

"Karma!"

"Go away. Begone!"

"Karma, wake up, boy! Time to get the tea ready."

Karma got up, flustered. Dawn was breaking. After seeing the goods train through, the pointsman was coming back, revolving the bamboo circle. Sala! What a horrible dream. He had never had such a nightmare in all the twelve years of his life.

Karma was not an employee of the Railway Company. If he wanted to, he could easily get the job of a pointsman, a porter or a water vendor. If it came to that, he could easily get in by the back door. But his heart was not in it. He had never liked the Railway Company's blue shirt with an engine engraved on its brass buttons.

For that matter, Karma did not relish the idea of getting a regular job, be it with the Railways or any other agency. When they asked what he did for a living, he replied that he kept company with the Railway babus. A man who received no regular wages could not be termed an employee. Could he? Not by a long shot.

He had stayed with Gopal Babu for five years. After that, he lived with many more babus. To tell their exact number, he would have to count on his fingers. But one thing, he always lived with Relief Babus – not with those who were permanent fixtures at one railway station or the other and lived in railway quarters with their families.

Gopal Babu – what a gem of a man! The like of whom he would never come across again. Gopal Babu was Karma's friend, mentor, mother, all rolled into one. Karma was unclaimed goods, without any tag or label. Gopal Babu had taken delivery of him from the railway hospital and had then taken him under his wings. Karma accompanied him wherever he went and partook of the same food with him. But one fine morning, Gopal Babu took it into his head to swap duties with a station babu. This was followed by another wild plunge. He got married. And what a wife! Was she a woman or a witch? The whole day Gopal Babu remained in full possession of his wits, but as evening approached, his heart started fluttering like a wounded sparrow. Sometimes at midnight, when he went out to flag the special train through on her onward journey, one felt that he had come from his quarters after stoking the boiler of a powerful Canadian locomotive.

Karma used to sleep in the verandah of the Babu's quarters, and rarely had a full night's uninterrupted sleep. Gopal Babu's wife would start puffing and ranting. Then followed groans, cries, abuses, ending in an exchange of blows. At last when the Babu tried to escape from the house, she would rush at him and pull him back by his hair. Then Karma hit upon a way of averting this rumpus. As the hour of midnight approached, he would start hammering on the door, shouting that the special train was due to pass through. But this strategy did not work for long. One day that bossy woman cried, "Drive away this bastard from my sight! He is a thief! A t – h – i – e – f!"

From that day, whenever Karma happened to pass by a railway quarter, a thin voice would start ringing in his ears. "Thief! Bastard!" Before the year was out, she had devoured Gopal Babu, flesh, bones and all. Gopal Babu, who was tender like a flower. The thought brought tears to Karma's eyes.

A wandering mendicant, flowing water and a Relief Babu – they know no rest.

As soon as a Relief Babu returned to the Headquarters, he would be urgently called back to replace such and such Babu at a particular station, who had suddenly taken ill. A Relief Babu had always to be on his toes. With even the best of luck, he could not hope to stay for more than three months at a stretch at one station. He carried his home in a wooden box. Here today, gone tomorrow.

Gopal Babu had himself put Karma onto Ghosh Babu, telling him that he was a good man and would take good care of him. But he could not put on with Ghosh Babu for more than a month. He had a foul tongue and was given to abusing all the time. Otherwise he was a nice fellow, without any other fault. To talk filth had become a habit with him. Even today, when he met Karma, he greeted him with an abuse: "How are you, Karma, you son of a …?"

Ram Babu too was not a bad sort either. He had a clean slate but one resetting sin – lust for women. Whichever station he was posted to, he would call the pointsman, the porter or the sweeper aside and get into a huddle with him, talking to him in a tell-tale jargon. At night, under cover of darkness, his shadowy figure was often found stalking around the godown, the ladies' waiting room or even the ladies' lavatory. How despicable of him! Like a refrain he had only one sentence on his lips all the lime: "Know of any good lay?" And then as Karma had feared, tragedy struck. A woman was his undoing. Last year, on the Jogbani line, a Gorkha chopped off his body into two pieces with his *khukhri.* That did it. He was paid back right and proper for going after women.

In utter contrast to him, Singhji was very devout. He always carried the images of Ram, Sita and Lakshman with him in his bag. His day started at four in the morning when he took his bath and sat down to pray, ringing the bell all the time. Nobody was allowed to enter the sanctum where the images were installed, without a bath. A worshipper was required to take a bath everytime he wanted to enter the sanctum, which was hard on Karma, particularly in winter. "What sacrilege!" Singhji would suddenly scream. "You have again touched the image!" Didn't the Railway Company know better than to employ such oddities? No wonder Karma did not last long with him.

Then there was Sahu Babu, as generous as he was fond of the bottle. Once, roaring drunk at daytime, he had blithely given clearance to a goods train which collided with an oncoming train on the same track. Karma vividly remembered that when Sahu Babu realised the enormity of his blunder, he made up for it by quickly downing one more bottle of country liquor. But surprisingly enough, he got away with it. The Railway Doctor declared that he had gone out of his mind.

But even on that night of the ghastly accident, Karma did not have such a horrible dream as he had last night. Of course he had been a fool to have narrated the dream to the Railway Babu so early in the morning. It could be taken as an ill omen. The Babu was new on the job and Karma had yet to size him up, specially as to his temperament. Although they had been together for a week, it was only last night that the Babu had opened out to him by asking a personal question or two. That had prompted Karma to unload the dream from his mind. As he handed him his morning cup of tea, the words tumbled from his mouth, "Babu, last night I had a strange dream. The hurtling engine, my body glued to the rail track, my head on this side of the track and my legs on the other side. And there was Anthony Guard Saheb's pair of gumboots."

"What rot are you talking?" the Babu had barked at him. "Are you addicted to *ganja?*"

Karma felt foolish. He shouldn't have talked to the Babu about his dream. Picking up the looking glass from the alcove, he studied his face in it. Oh, god, what was wrong with his lips? They looked like the beak of a partridge.

"Karam Chand, what's wrong with you?"

Oh, there goes the bell. The train is coming and my pot of vegetables is still on the *chulha.* But what's going on here? Why is the shunting engine hauling this train? And what a thin whistle! Like a Santhali flute's sound. Si-i-i.

Karma had lived at the Maniharighat station too. It is a magnificent station, a huge affair, completely dwarfing the midget station of Amadpura.

Whenever he went to a new station, Karma liked to go out on a ramble to the countryside around. Without that he felt sort of bottled up. On his rambles he met many people, visited many places. He remembered the mangoes of Sonbasa, the fish of Kaluchak, the curds of Bhatoia and the sugarcane of Kusiagram. But most of all he remembered the Maniharighat station. On one side, the land, and on the other, a vast stretch of water. On one side, the train, and on the other, a steam boat. Then there were fields, the blue waters and a white sandy stretch merging into the blue range of hills of Sahebgunj.

Karma had bathed in the holy waters of the Ganga for full four months. For four lives, no curse would ever work on him.

No other station had such a beautiful name. Maniharighat. God bless the name.

Mastan Babu originally belonged to the labour class and started life as a coolie at the Maniharighat station. Soon he was overcome by despondency and lost interest in life. He grew a beard, kept long hair and turned a sadhu. He played on castanets and sang devotional songs. One *chillum* of ganja put enough strength in him to carry him through five cycles of devotional songs. Karma had picked up a few snatches of devotional songs from him, but he never touched ganja. So when the Babu asked him if he had taken ganja, his memory suddenly harked back to the days when he used to attend the devotee Babu's hymn-singing sessions.

Karma again took the looking glass from the alcove and looked at his face in it. He screwed up his eyes and baring his teeth in a smile he aped Mastan Babu. "Be happy!" he raised his hands to bless. "Keep your eyes and ears open. The earth also speaks and the trees and plants recognise people. Haven't you ever seen the crop singing and dancing? Or seen it crying on a dark moonless night? Ha, ha! Remain happy!"

He did not know that the Babu was standing behind him, watching his antics.

"So you dream even while standing," the Babu said, "and then you tell me that you don't smoke ganja."

True, he had been day dreaming. Mastan Babu's face had started growing bigger like a banyan tree and his mad laughter went ringing through the sky while whiffs of ganja smoke blew in the air. There was a tide in the Ganga. Far off, the hooter of a steamboat blew – long and drawn out.

"Serve the food," the Babu said. "Let me see what it tastes like. You drive me mad."

The Babu swallowed the first morsel, smacked his lips and fixed his eyes on Karma's face. "It tastes nice," he said. The food had suddenly put him in good humour. "Who taught you to cook? Gopal Babu's wife?"

"You mean, *Bo-ma?*" Karma said "Oh, no. She only knew how to abuse. Her tongue was so bitter that even the milk on the boil curdled. She was a vulgar woman."

"And who taught you to wag your tongue?"

Suddenly Karma remembered Mastan Babu's words. "Babu, who teaches whom?" he said looking very thoughtful. "The police station sets the pace of the town."

"Your spouse will deem herself lucky," the Babu said after a pause.

Karma decided that if the Babu's good mood lasted, he would tell him Mastan Babu's story with a few songs thrown in for good measure.

"Babu, today I want to take some time off."

"Why, are you going somewhere?"

Karma raised his hand and pointed his finger towards the door. "I'll go out and walk and walk and walk."

If only he could have somebody by his side.

"Your spouse will deem herself lucky," Babu's words rang in his ears.

Karma's wife. Warisganj station. The nomads camping in their tents outside the station. And that girl fast growing up into a woman, a nosegay scintillating in her nostril, her yellow teeth glinting scarlet red with tooth paint.

Karma lacked the courage to regale that lass with *halwa* and *puris*, prepared with his own loving hands. One day he had taken them to her, wrapped up in a sheet of newspaper. But he got soaking wet with perspiration and his nerve failed him at the last moment. What if the girl got scared and raised a cry that he was trying to seduce her with halwa and puri?

Even after he had crossed the railway yard, the dog kept following him. Karma was annoyed. "Go back," he cried. "Don't stir out that far. Other dogs will pounce on you and tear you to bits. Go back! Go!"

The dog stopped and watched Karma walking along the narrow path cutting through the paddy fields. The ears of rice had not yet sprouted. Suddenly he remembered Chaudhry Babu's pregnant wife. It was said that the lady doctor had taken a photograph of the inside of her and proclaimed that she had twins in her womb.

The rains had been good that season. The paddy fields were still flooded with rain water. And what fishes!

Karma's body stiffened as his eyes fell on *magur* fish. For some time he stood there watching them with bated breath and then he slowly squelched his way towards the abutment. The water which had looked like a solid sheet of glass suddenly rippled. Karma stood there fascinated. If only he could upturn the water like a sheet over one of the abutments.

"Hey! Hey! Stop wriggling and twisting. You are done for now. You can't escape. Karma is an old hand at this game."

Eight *magurs* and one *girayi.* All jet black. He could easily get three rupees for the lot at the Katihar fish market. Pleased, Karma securely tied the fish in his gamchha.

The palm tree gradually kept receding till, with the first whiff of smell, Karma realised that he was already in the village. His eyes alighted on a man who was tending his cabbage patch. His hair had gone gray, but the muscles of his arms rippled as he watered the field. They recognised each other. He was the man who had recently come to the station to despatch his bag of brinjals.

"Bhai, what brings you here?" he asked Karma.

"I've come out for a walk in the countryside. Do you live in this village?"

The old man laughed and his thick bristly moustache quivered, reminding Karma of ticket collector Sattu Babu's old father.

A girl wearing a red sari came holding a hookah. Her cheeks puffed out as she blew at the chillum to keep the hookah going. She momentarily slopped on seeing Karma and then resumed her walk, picking her way through the cabbage patch.

"Beti, go back," the old man said. "We are coming to the house."

"Who's he, Babu?" the girl looked at Karma.

"The bear man."

"Hisht!"

Karma felt embarrassed and looked away. Did he really look like a bear man?

"You're Relief Babu's servant, aren't you?" the old man asked.

"No, not a servant. I just live with him. That's all."

"What do you mean live with him? How much are you paid?"

"Nothing. Why should he pay me for doing nothing?"

For a while the old man kept looking at Karma, forgetting that he was holding the stem of the hookah. "You mean nothing? You work for free for him?"

He looked towards the courtyard. "Saraswatia!" he called out. "Send your mother down here. I have a wonderful fellow with me. Let her have a look at him."

An old woman who was standing behind the curtain quickly stepped across the door.

"Look at this young chap," the old man said. "He works for a handful of rice. Do they give you clothes also?" he turned to Karma.

"What's your name? Karmachand? A nice name, indeed. But you didn't tell me what you do for a living."

"Your brinjals look excellent," Karma said, evading the old man's question. "They must be delicious like ghee."

The old woman smiled. Her smile seemed to have revived Karma, sending a new surge of strength through his body.

"Stop rubbing the poor fellow the wrong way," she said turning to her husband. "Let him have a breather."

"What's there in your gamchha?" the old man asked. "Fish? For your Babu?"

"I just caught them on the way," Karma said.

"Saraswatia's mother," the old man turned to his wife. "Get some parched rice. Let our guest eat it with fish curry. It will go well with parched rice. Young man, for a change, sample the taste of fish curry cooked by other hands. Saraswatia's mother will cook it for you."

While he was eating, Karma heard someone asking the old woman, "Saraswatia's ma, where has your guest come from?"

"From Katihar."

"Who is he?"

"A relative."

"Have never heard of any relative of yours at Katihar."

Karma looked up. Saraswatia was standing in the distance, blowing on a chillum, her cheeks looking round like sweet limes.

The old man asked in a voice oozing with affection, "Boy, what makes a man's voice travel through telephone poles? I just want to know that." When he was about to leave, the old woman stopped Karma. "Don't take the old man amiss," she said. "His son died in the bloom of youth. Since then he has become a little loose in the head."

"Come again someday."

"Regard it as your own home."

To Karma's surprise, the dog was still there, waiting for him. It expressed its joy by cutting a few capers and then bursting into speed. When Karma entered the railway compound, he realised to his chagrin that he had been diddled by the old man. Three rupees worth of *magur* fish was gone in exchange for a handful of parched rice, a helping of fish curry and a few honeyed words. He felt he had betrayed the Babu too. The sight of fish would have made him delirious with joy.

The other Babu had arrived with his family by the night train. The railway quarter which was usually quiet had suddenly burst into life. Karma's Babu would be leaving for the Headquarters by the morning train. Karma would go with him. And then onto Maniharighat.

Karma lay down to sleep, though he knew sleep would not come easily to him, unlike the Babu who always slept like a log, having no particular attachment for any place.... Come again some day.... Regard it as your own home. The words kept echoing in Karma's mind, but he did not know what to make of them. Did he have any home?

Suddenly a strange smell assailed his nostrils. He got up to find out where the smell was coming from and slowly walked across the platform, following the smell. As he stepped on to the rail track, all the signals – home point and distant – suddenly blazed forth. A woman shrieked from one of the quarters, "Thief! Thief!" Karma fled, an engine in hot pursuit of him. And that nomad's daughter. He hid in her tent. Saraswatia burst into a hearty laughter. Her golden hair and the smell of her unwashed body becoming one with Karma. Scared, he hid his face in Saraswatia's, no, her mother's lap.

"Karma, get up! Karma, carry the luggage out."

Karma, who had been wallowing in a sea of smells got up, flustered, and reached for his shirt.

The train came. The Babu hurriedly got into a carriage. Karma helped him with the luggage and then got into the servant's compartment.

"Have you put in all the luggage?" the Babu shouted to him from his carriage. "Are you sure you have left nothing behind?"

The engine whistled. Karma saw that the dog was sitting on the platform, whining, its eyes fixed on Karma. The dog looked so restless.

"Babu!"

"Yes?"

"I won't go."

Karma jumped down as the train started moving. He stumbled as his feet hit the platform. But the next moment, he had steadied himself.

2

Yet Another Life

Mohan Rakesh

Mohan Rakesh, an outstanding name in Hindi fiction, was born in 1925. He received his education at Hindu College, Amritsar, and at the Oriental College, Lahore. He lived and worked for some time in Bombay, New Delhi and Jalandhar. Thereafter, he adopted writing as an independent profession and devoted his entire time to it. For a year, he also edited *Sarika.* He has published six collections of short stories, two novels and three plays. His stories set a new trend in Hindi writing and he received great acclaim as a playwright. He also won the Sangeet Natak Akademi Award. He was also awarded the Jawaharlal Nehru Fellowship before he died in 1972.

For a moment Prakash felt that his heart-beat had stopped. What a moment! It had the impact of a meteor hitting the earth. Searing the heart of the billowing fog, the moment spent itself out.

He again looked closely at the passing figures outlined in the fog. Could a man's eyes deceive so outrageously? Was it an illusion or a reality?

For the past many days, his eyes had roved over the road just to spot out those figures. He thought he could even make out the green of the sari's *pallu* and the blue of the shorts; as if he had been looking for just those two colours in the vast expanse of the fog. In fact, till they came right under his balcony, he had taken these two figures for casual passers-by. Then recognition came in a flash, like a thought suddenly released from the subconscious mind in an unguarded moment.

The figure in blue shorts turned to look back as if it was also searching for someone in the fog. Prakash wanted to call out, but no sound came from his throat. In the glum quiet of the sea of fog, his speechlessness was like the silence of a storm, bottled up within itself for want of air.

He returned to his room. The room was in disarray. He frowned and made a half-hearted effort to search for something. Was this the kind of life he had been looking forward to? He couldn't even think coherently. His eyes landed on the trousers hanging from the wall. Pulling off his pyjamas he got into the trousers and stood undecided for a moment.

His hand fell on the lock lying on the table and that decided it. Quickly locking up the room, he descended the stairs. On the stairs he realised that he had forgotten to put on his shoes. But he decided against going back to the room. As he stepped into the street, his feet landed in mud, spattering his trousers. He peered into the distance and saw that the two figures had almost reached the pony stand. Asking a passing horseman to run up and stop that child in blue shorts, he hurried after him. The horseman broke into a trot and rushed past the two figures without stopping. He seemed to have conveyed his message to the wrong persons.

Even though walking at a brisk pace, Prakash felt as if his knees had grown stiff and he was not walking fast enough. Even the distance seemed to have become longer and he feared that those people would go away before he caught up with them.

He suddenly stopped a few yards from them. Should he take the plunge?

"Palash!" He called. The word seemed to have escaped his lips despite himself.

The child's big eyes suddenly turned in his direction and with him, his mother's. There was surprise in the child's eyes and he clung to his mother.

"Palash, come to me!" Prakash clicked his fingers almost as though it were an everyday affair with him to accost the child.

The child looked at his mother. But finding her looking away, he clung closer to her.

Prakash stood there confused, as if he had come all the way just to measure the distance. Then he walked up and lifted the child in his arms. The child perked up and tried to wriggle out of his grasp. But the next moment he threw his tiny arms round his neck and started hugging him.

"Didn't you recognise your Papa?" Prakash asked him.

"Yes, I did," the child lisped and hugged him again.

"Then why didn't you come to me at once?"

"Just like that!" The child suddenly kissed his cheek.

"Did you arrive this morning?"

"No. We came yesterday."

"Will you stay for some days or go back today?"

"I'll be here for three or four days.

"You'll come to meet your Papa, won't you?"

Pressing the child against him, Prakash kissed his cheek. Overwhelmed, the child kissed him first on his forehead and then on his cheek.

"Look at that child!" A Kashmiri labourer who was standing by, looked at them, amused.

"Where do you stay?" The child held back his face from Prakash's to have a better view of him.

"Over there." Prakash pointed his finger towards the balcony.

"When'll you come?"

"Now, I'll go back and have my milk," the child looked at his mother. "After that. I'll come to you."

"I'll sit in the balcony and wait for you." Prakash's eyes met the mother's for a fleeting moment and then looked away. Getting down from Prakash's lap, the child ran up and clung to his mothers' legs.

"But we're going to Khilanmarg," she said, looking beyond the fog at the hazy outlines of deodars.

"No, I won't go to Khilanmarg," the child said in a decisive voice. "I'll go to my Papa after I drink my milk."

The sky had remained overcast the past three days, as if painted over with a thick coat of white zinc. As time passed, the fog become more opaque and assuming many shapes, billowed about, as if trying to find its own depth. The balcony looked suspended in the air, having an isolated existence of its own. In the distance, tops of deodars jutted out, here and there, forming a green line resembling a hazy script inscribed against the misty sky. Prakash watched it tensely, as if trying to save it from getting obliterated. When the line was finally gone, he threw back his head in defeat. As he sat there, he recalled a day out of his past, four years ago, still vivid in his memory.

It was his child's first birthday – the day that drove the final wedge between him and his wife.

Owing to incompatibility of temperament, they had started living apart only a few months after their marriage. They were now working separately. They met once in six months, just to keep up appearances. It was this pretence of keeping up appearances that had tricked them into bringing the child into the world. Bina, his wife, suspected that she had deliberately been made to walk into a trap, while Prakash thought it was the result of an inadvertent mistake.

As the child's birthday approached, Bina invited Prakash to come over to Lucknow, where she was going to celebrate the event at her father's place.

In reply, Prakash sent her a telegram saying that he would run up to Lucknow for a day and stay with a friend at Hazratganj.

The party, he suggested, should be held at his friend's place where he had already invited some other friends.

He looked forward to meeting Bina at the railway station. But she was not there. Then he sent her word to come to the party with the child. The evening merged into night but Bina did not come. Later on he learnt, to his chagrin, that she was having a party of her own at her father's house.

He did not sleep the whole night. In the morning, he sent her a message. This time she turned up with the child and they kept squabbling till late in the night.

"Bina, don't forget, I'm his father. I have a right over him."

"It's only an accident that you're his father," Bina replied. "If you had a father's heart you would have come to the party."

"Bina! I don't understand! Have you thought of the effect of all this on the child?"

"When we can't think straight about ourselves, how can we think about the child?"

"I'll keep the child."

"Entrust the child to you?" Bina said in a bitter tone. "Forget it! I can't leave him, to the uncertainties of tomorrow. I'm not so stupid!"

"Then I'll have to seek legal redress."

"By all means. I have no objection. I'll fight to the bitter end."

Many months passed and he was still pondering the matter. Could a man wipe out his past like a bad dream and begin life anew on a clean slate? After all, a man was given only one life. It was up to him to love it well or gamble it away on experiments. But did a wrong experiment mean that he had reached the point of no return?

While he was signing the papers in the courtroom, a sparrow struck the ceiling fan and fell; hurt, on the floor.

Days, weeks and months passed.

Even after two-and-a-half years Prakash had not been able to make a new start in life. During this long period, the child had visited him only thrice. Each time, he came with a servant, and went away at nightfall. On the first visit, he was shy and withdrawn, but later he became chummy. Prakash would take him out for a walk, feed him ice cream and buy him toys. When the time for parting came, the child would refuse to leave. "I'll have milk before I go, I'll also stay for dinner," he would insist.

On the third visit, when the child stayed late with him, a stranger came to look for him. The child was silting on his father's knee, eating his dinner. "Don't you see he's eating his dinner?"

"Let him finish his meal," the man said icily. "I'll wait downstairs." When the child was gone, Prakash discovered that he had forgotten his cap behind. He ran down into the street with the cap. Besides the stranger and the servant, there was one more person there – the child's mother. They were walking about fifty yards ahead of him. When he called after them, the four of them turned to look. Then the servant came back to take the cap while the others dismissed him from their minds and walked on, unconcerned. Prakash was deeply hurt.

The question arose afresh in his mind: why not tear himself off from his past and set up a new home? But he was always tormented by doubts. How did he know that he would not fail a second time? He saw the shadow of his past failure writ large on the face of every girl he thought eligible. He had a sneaking fear that his marriage would again founder on the rocks unless the girl was the exact opposite of Bina. Bina was highly educated, proud and earned more than him. She had an exaggerated notion of her independence and felt that she could cope with every situation by herself. Even physically she was tougher and had a touch of the masculine about her. Prakash wanted a wife who was prepared to play second fiddle to him.

Nirmala, the sister of his friend, Krishan Juneja, was one such girl. He had met her casually on a few occasions. Simple and modestly educated. Though twenty-six, she did not look more than eighteen. The Junejas were not well off. Perhaps that was why the girl had remained unmarried for so long. When the question of her marriage with him was broached, he readily agreed. He was hoping to put his life back on the rails.

Nirmala came to her new home with a smile on her face. He found her smiling all the time. The smile came without any reason and showed no sign of leaving. Prakash felt peeved. Even kids didn't laugh the way she did. If a thing fell on the floor, she would start laughing and did not stop for minutes. He tried to make her understand the fatuity of laughing over trifles but it only invited more laughter. When he spoke sharply, she became grouchy, pulled her hair, and, lying down in bed, started kicking and muttering, pretending that she was a *devi* and had the power to put his whole faimly under a curse. Sometimes she ripped off her clothes and hid them in the house. She even hid jewellery in shoes and other unlikely places. At other times, she would complain of abscesses on her body and would groan for days. Then she would suddenly get well, as if by a miracle, take to washing the laundry and keep at it the whole day.

When she was in a slightly better frame of mind, her face became round, she looked very sweet and she started sucking her thumb.

Prakash saw Nirmala in many moods, and the more he saw of her, the more he felt that he had been pushed into a blind alley, from which there was no escape. While walking on the road, his mind would start wandering, and he would stop in his tracks, trying to remember where he had come from and where he was going.

He was angry at Juneja for having diddled him in such a crass manner. Nirmala's proper place was in the mental hospital. Why was she palmed off on him? He wrote to Juneja many times, but got no reply. Then he went to meet him and was told curtly that Nirmala was his wife. Her brothers had no business to poke their noses in others' private lives. He must sort it out with Nirmala as best he can.

"Why did you go to my brothers?" Nirmala demanded, her hair dishevelled. "Do you want to divorce me like Bina and take another wife? But I'm not Bina, I'm a devoted wife. If you ever take it into your head to desert me, I'll reduce your house to ashes. I have the power to rock your house. Do you want to have an earthquake? Well, look!" She spread out her arms. "Come, earthquake, come, come, came!"

Prakash tried to calm her. "Don't lay your dirty hands on me." She exploded. "I'm a chaste woman. Did I ever marry you? I'm still a child. No man on earth dare touch me. Touch me and see what happens!"

At his wits' end, Prakash shut himself up in his room.

"Papa!"

Prakash got up from his chair and looked below, wondering if it was Palash's voice that he had heard. His eyes travelled to the Tourist Hotel in the distance, but he saw no one resembling Palash. Disappointed, he again sat down in the chair.

"Papa!"

Prakash looked down, startled. It was the same fog and the same quiet road. A Kashmiri was laboriously trudging up the road. Was he imagining things!

Just then, the sound of footsteps fell on his ears. Simultaneously, two tiny arms clung round his heck and soft curly hair brushed his lips.

"Papa!"

"May I go, Palash?" It was a forgotten but familiar voice. Prakash looked round. Bina was standing outside his room, her eyes fixed on some object."

"Oh! You!" Holding the child in his arms. Prakash quickly rose from his chair. "Won't you come in?"

"I must go," Bina didn't look at him. "I just wanted to know when you will send him back to me."

"Any time you want him." Prakash came towards the stairs.

"He has his glass of milk at four."

"Then I'll send him back by four."

"Should I leave a pullover for him? He has only a light sweater on."

"Yes, please do."

Bina held out a pullover from across the threshold.

"And you...?" Prakash wanted her to come into the room, but the words died in his throat. He followed her as she walked towards the stairs. "Please don't feed him ice cream," she said from the stairs. "It is bad for his throat." For an instant, Bina hesitated at the top of the stairs and then quickly walked down.

"Papa! Can I have ice cream?" the child asked, throwing his arms round Prakash's neck when Bina was gone.

"Yes, son," Prakash fondled the child. "Eat what you like."

Then, as if suddenly forgetting himself and the child, he kept peering into the fog.

The curtain of fog lifted slowly, defining the greenery stretching for miles around. They were walking across the golf course towards the club.

"Papa, why has a man got two legs? Why not four?"

"Arre!" Prakash looked at him startled.

"What do you mean, 'arre'?"

"I did't know you can talk so distinctly. Why do you lisp all the time?" Lifting him in his arms, Prakash brought his face close. The child started laughing. It had an echo of his own laughter and he saw in him his own face as it was thirty years back.

"Mummy likes my talking with a lisp."

"Why?"

"I don't know. Ask her."

"Does your Mummy also object to your laughing loudly?"

He remembered the days when, annoyed at his uproarious laughter, Bina used to cover her ears with her hands.

"Yes," the child said, firmly grasping Prakash's neck. "Mummy says good boys don't laugh like that."

Prakash pul him down on the ground and held his hand.

"Papa," the child said, "Why don't good boys laugh loudly?"

"There's no harm in it. All good boys laugh heartily."

"Then why does Mummy object?"

"She won't object anymore. And don't speak with a lisp."

They walked some distance in silence. Then the child asked, "Papa, why didn't you come to my birthday party? Mummy said you didn't come because you were away in England."

"Yes, that's true."

"Don't go to England again."

"Why?"

"I don't like your going away. Your face, too, has changed."

Prakash gave a hollow laugh. "In what way has my face changed?"

"I don't know. But it looks different. Earlier it was not like that. Now it's different."

"Different how?"

"I don't know. Your hair was black. Now it has turned grey."

"You didn't come to live with me. That's why it has turned grey."

"How could I?" the child laughed so loudly that he almost lost his balance. "You were in England. How could I go there? Could I go there by myself?"

"Yes, you could. You've grown big now."

"Of course I'm big, am I not, Papa?" He clapped his hands. "Tell mummy about it. She says I'm still very small. I'm not small, am I?"

"No, you're not small." Prakash started running. "Catch me!" he said. The child ran after him, throwing out his tiny legs. Prakash was again reminded of his childhood. "How the kid throws out his legs!"

"Papa, why is the grass green? Why isn't if red?"

Prakash had hired a pony for the child and was now walking by his side on the bridle road to Khilanmarg. The child was watching with keen eyes the scene around him and the velvety grass under him, on which the fog lay heavy like spent passion. As impulse seized him, he jumped in the saddle and tugged at the reins.

"Everything has it's own special colour," Prakash said, tenderly pinching the child's thigh.

"Why has everything its own special colour?"

"Because nature has made it so."

"What's nature?"

Prakash bent down and kisssed his thigh. "That's what they call nature," he said.

The child laughed. "You're telling a lie," he said.

"What makes you say so?"

"Because you don't know the answer."

"Then you tell me why the grass is green."

"It grows out of the earth. That's why it's green."

"Really! How do you know?"

The child jumped in his saddle and lugged at the rein. "Mummy told me," he replied.

Prakash's lips curled up in a thin smile. He felt he was still squabbling with Bina and she was getting the better of him.

"What else has your Mummy told you?" he asked. "Has she told you why man has only two legs, not four?"

"Yes. Mummy said, man has only two legs because half of him walks on earth and other half in the air."

"I didn't know that." A faint smile played across Prakash's face and then he became grave.

"Papa, you know nothing about anything," the child said. "You've grown so big and yet you know nothing."

The grass, the snow and the sky changed colours many times in the day, and with them changed Prakash's moods. On waking up in the morning, he would go on to the balcony and keep looking towards the Tourist Hotel, waiting for the child's visit. He went out only to snatch a hurried breakfast and lunch, lest the child should turn away in his absence.

That morning when he saw the child coming with his mother, he rushed down into the street. But instead of coming to him, the child disappeared into the nearby photographer's studio with his mother. After waiting for some time, Prakash went back to his room, hoping that the child would come up to him of his own accord. Standing in his balcony, he saw that instead of coming to him, the child was dragging his mother towards the Tourist Hotel. In the evening, when he could not hold himself in patience any longer, he bought some cherries and proceeded towards the hotel. From a distance he saw the child emerging from the hotel with his mother. As his eyes landed on Prakash, he ran back into the hotel.

Prakash stopped in his tracks. His eyes met Bina's. Her complexion had become a shade darker and there were rings under her eyes. She looked thinner than before.

He stood undecided for a moment and then walking up to her held the bag of cherries before her. "They are for the child," he said. His throat was parched.

Avoiding his gaze, Bina took the bag from him.

"Palash!" she called out in a firm voice. "Look, Papa has brought cherries for you."

"I don't want them!" The child peeped from the lobby and then ran back.

Bina looked at Prakash and then at the child's receding figure. Prakash went into the hotel, and chasing the child, picked him up in his arms.

"I won't speak with you." The child made frantic efforts to get down from his arms.

"No, child," Prakash said, making clucking sounds. "Does one ever get angry with one's Papa?"

"Why didn't you come into the shop to see my photographs?"

"Which photographs? I knew nothing about them."

A young woman standing by Bina's side, of whom Prakash had taken no notice till now, explained that the child, eager to show him his photographs, had gone into the studio to fetch them. But before he came back, he was gone.

"All right, I'll see them now," Prakash said. "And then I'll take you for a stroll."

"But Mummy must come with me," the child said, perking up in Prakash's arms.

"Yes, she'll come with us." Prakash looked at Bina. She bit her lip and followed them into the studio.

The photographer spread out the photographs on the counter. "Look Papa," the child said, picking up a photograph. "It gives a full view of Kashmir. And this one," he said picking up another, "shows me on horseback."

After having finished seeing the photographs, Prakash came out of the studio holding the child's hand. He heard Bina calling after them. "Are you taking him for a stroll?"

Prakash looked back at her. "I'll bring him back in a short while."

"I just wanted to say one thing."

"Yes?"

Bina stood thinking for a moment. "Don't tell him anything which may..."

Prakash went numb. He lowered his eyes.

"Where are we going, Papa?" the child asked.

"To the club. I'll hire a pony for you."

That night, after many days, Prakash had a sound and dreamless sleep. Even so, when he woke up in the morning, he did not feel fresh; he had a sense of emptiness inside him.

Last night when he went to sleep, it had been raining heavily. But now the sky was clear and the hills in the distance looked brilliant in the sun. Then his mind suddenly darkened like clouds gathering against the horizon and a vague fear clutched his heart. Last evening, the child had dropped a casual hint that if the sky cleared, his Mummy may go away in the morning.

Slowly the morning merged into afternoon and the child did not come. He recoiled at the thought of the child coming to bid him goodbye and wished that the evening should also approach in the same unobtrusive manner and sink into the night. But when the afternoon was also gone and the child did not turn up, he felt concerned. Had they left in the morning?

He decided to go to Tourist Hotel and find out for himself. He was going up the road when he saw the child and Bina standing under his balcony. He walked back in long strides. When he held the child's arm, he wrenched his arm free and refused to take notice of him.

"I'll not go to your house," he whimpered.

Taken aback, Prakash let the child go and stood aside, embarrassed.

"Are you angry with me?" he asked without looking at the child or Bina.

"I won't go up unless Mummy comes with me," he cried.

The parents' eyes met and slid away.

"Why don't you also come up?" Prakash then asked in a matter-of-fact voice.

"I don't know what's the matter with him," Bina said testily. "He's not himself since morning."

"He won't go up without you," Prakash said in a colourless tone. "Don't you see how adamant he is?"

"Come, I'll leave you on the stairs," Bina said. "And don't take long. The horses are ready."

The words stabbed, but he immediately regained his composure. "Are you leaving today?" he asked in a staid tone, trying not to give himself away.

"Yes," Bina replied, still looking the other way. "I wanted to leave in the morning. But this child is getting too much for me. Even now..."

Bina blinked, and gave Prakash a sharp, troubled look. "Let's go up," she said picking up the child.

The child's scowl suddenly changed into a smile and he threw his arms round his mother's neck. Prakash climbed the stairs ahead of them.

Quickly removing the knick-knacks lying on the chair, he pushed it towards Bina. But she sat down on the edge of the bed. Suddenly something attracted the child's attention and he ran into the balcony.

Prakash stood there holding the back of the chair and Bina, withdrawing into herself, stared at the wall.

Their eyes met in an unguarded moment. Concentrating all her strength at one point, Bina said: "Yesterday I found some money in the child's pocket. Did you give it to him?"

"Yes," Prakash said haltingly. "Buy him something."

Bina was silent for a while.

"What thing?" she asked at last.

"Anything. Maybe an overcoat."

Another silence.

"What kind of overcoat?"

"Any kind. I leave it to you."

"Any special cloth?"

"Any cloth will do."

"Any particular colour?"

"No...well, how about blue?"

Then Prakash suddenly remembered that Bina disliked blue, and he regretted having mentioned that colour.

The child came prancing into the room.

"Let's go," he said, holding his mother's hand.

"You haven't even given Papa a kiss," Prakash lifted him in his arms. The child hastily kissed Prakash and getting down from his lap, tugged at his mother's sari. Bina got up from the bed.

"Let's go, Mummy." The child dragged her towards the door.

"You'll write to your Papa, won't you? Prakash called after him.

"Yes, sure." The child replied without looking back. Then he saw Bina turning to look at him. But she immediately shifted her gaze to hide the tears hovering over her lashes.

"Say ta-ta to Papa," she said, pulling her hand on the child's shoulder. "Ta-ta, Papa!" The child waved his hand without looking back at his father and started walking down the stairs. When he was halfway down, Prakash again heard his voice. "Papa's house is no good. Mummy, our house is good. There arc not many things in Papa's house."

"Ssh! Quiet!" Bina reproved him. "You blurt out whatever comes into your mind.

"I won't keep, quiet. No, I won't," the child said in a tearful voice. "Papa's house is like spit."

"One more hand – and that'll be the last." His own voice sounded unfamiliar to Prakash. His friends agreed after a half-hearted refusal. The cards were dealt.

The card room had emptied and the fire in the grate had died down long ago. A few embers shuddering in the cold, were fast sinking into the ash.

Prakash picked up his cards. They were odd again and he felt like throwing them down in disgust. But having asked to continue the game, he could not now back out, and studied his cards gloomily.

It was raining in torrents; the downpour was heavier than last night. The rain drops struck against the window-panes with a staccato warning and then helplessly slid down, making vague patterns. They looked like faces set against the glass, shedding incessant tears. The doors rattled with the wind, the faces sobbed. Then they stopped sobbing and frowned in anger.

Behind those faces lay thick darkness where something seemed to be gasping for life.

"Declare!" Prakash looked up startled. This time again he had to throw down a full hand. Settling back, he started staring at the faces peering from behind the window-panes.

"Prakash, you're a lucky guy – the luckiest of us all!" Prakash shifted, his gaze from the window-pane. The cards had been put away and heads were bent over the table, adding up the scores.

"Haven't you heard: Unlucky at cards, lucky in love!" his companion said. "You're the biggest loser. A lucky guy indeed!"

Prakash read the amount written against his name. His heart started pounding as he drew the money from his pocket. After squaring up his account, he was left with two small coins and an inland letter which had come by the evening mail. Nirmala's letter. It had got crumpled in his pocket, unread. As he looked at his address scrawled across the page, many faces leapt up before his eyes. Each pen stroke was a face by itself – faces that laughed, cried, shrieked. And there were others, so gnome-like and hungry, that they looked as though they would gobble him up.

When he was collecting his things for the journey, Nirmala had a row with him.

"Nirmala!" he had said in dismay. "Stop it. Women don't wrestle. It's so humiliating."

"What's humiliating about it?" Nirmala had laughed. "Men and women wrestle day and night."

At last, he left with the clothes he stood in. He couldn't even take an extra shirt for the journey. He had to purchase all the things on the way to Kashmir. He didn't even have the time to think as to how long the five hundred rupees he had on him would last.

Nirmala had managed to get his address from a friend and there was a spate of letters from the fourth day of his arrival in Kashmir. These letters reflected the gamut of her facial contortions. She was terribly ill, she complained in one letter, and was seeking admission to a hospital. In another she wrote that her brothers had lodged a report with the police to trace their missing brother-in-law. Then she wrote that she had decided to become a *jogin* and live in the jungles. She threatened that if she did not hear from him, her brothers would despatch her to him on a plane. In another letter she complained that her younger brother had thrashed her for not living with her "bed-companion".

Prakash put the crumpled letter back into his pocket and rose from his chair. A few people were standing in the lobby, waiting for the rain to stop.

Edging his way through them, he came on the verandah steps.

"Going out in this rain?" one of than asked.

Ignoring the warning, he quickly stepped down the footpath. In front of him the lights on Nedou's Hotel shone palely through the surrounding darkness. Walking across the club compound, he came on to the road. The downpour had become heavier.

He was drenched and the rain was streaming over his body. His hands and feet had become numb with cold. When his mud-smeared shoes squelched in the puddles, a chill ran through his spine. Then his body tingled with a new sensation. He fell he was not alone on the road. Anotha person, throwing out tiny legs was plodding by his side. He looked back while crossing the wooden bridge. A wet dog was walking alongside him, flapping its ears every now and then. Mute and miserably stupid.

3

The City of Death

Amarkant

Amarkant was born in the Ballia district of Uttar Pradesh in 1925 and was educated at the Allahabad University. His stories, which mostly deal with middle-class society, are marked by deep insight, compassion and a tantalizing streak of satire. With four collections of short stories and half a dozen novels, he has carved a permanent place for himself in Hindi fiction.

Stepping out of his house, Ram craned his neck like a crow and looked up and down the lane. The sky, vaulted over like a neat blue tent, shed a soft light over the treetops, the roofs of the houses and over the park in front. By this time the mohalla used to come alive with a soft buzzing sound and shrill laughter. But today, no women or children were to be seen around. Only an eerie silence like a coiled serpent ready to strike. People stood in twos and threes in front of same houses, talking in hushed tones like conspirators.

Ram was a middle-aged man, short and small-built, his eyes red-rimmed and swollen, his shirt torn at one shoulder, his trousers crumpled and looking like a pair of slept-in pyjamas. He looked at the sky and sighed deeply.

He walked a few steps and then stopped, fear creeping over his face. As he stood there straining hard to listen, a noise drifted in from the direction of a mohalla on his left accompanied by cries of "Kill! Kill!" A loud palter of feet and then he saw some people running towards him. Should he run back into his house? He fell back a couple of steps. The people standing in front of their houses had not moved; they were still standing there and talking as before. Feeling a bit reassured, he tried to make out what the hubbub was about. Dogs! Dogs barking and fighting in the next mohalla. So even dogs were now flying at one another's throats! He tried to smile, but the smile died on his face like a burst bubble.

It was going to be eight. The curfew had been lifted after many days – four hours in the morning and the same period of time in the afternoon.

"Be careful!" Ram's wife had warned him in a beseeching tone as he stepped out of the house.

What did she mean? Who wanted her advice? Wasn't he already scared enough?

"So you want that something should happen to me?" he barked at her.

His wife had started sobbing and he had felt sorry at his rudeness, especially when he was leaving the house after many days. But sentiments had no place in an atmosphere of fear; they were swept away like pebbles before onrushing flood waters.

Further on, two people joined Ram which appeared to be pre-arranged and they resumed their walk. Their faces looked pinched and they cast furtive glances at one another as they walked, as if they had committed a crime and were afraid of being found out.

"Any news?" one of them asked in a muffled voice.

"They stabbed a man near the railway station," the other replied.

"A Hindu?"

"No, a Mohommedan."

"Is it true that they have found the dead body of a girl in Himmatganj?"

"Yes."

"A Mohommedan?"

"No, a Hindu."

Ram wordlessly listened to their talk and felt as if someone was twisting his heart and squeezing it dry of blood.

They had come to the end of the lane from where a brick wall took off and ran along the entire length of the next lane, obviously in an attempt to keep people apart, but it did not seem to have worked. They had pulled the bricks out in many places, making holes for people to pass through to the other side where a Muslim mohalla began. After Independence, the people of both the mohallas had started living in amity, the Hindus buying milk from Muslim *gowalas* and the Muslims, provisions on credit from *bania* shops. They joined in marriages and played cricket and football matches against one another.

Only two years ago, Jameel, a boy from the Muslim mohalla had become very popular in Ram's mohalla. Fond of music and drama, he had played the role of Subhadra in 'Veer Abhimanyu' – a mythological play – and was so much taken up with his role that while lamenting Abhimanyu's death, he had collapsed six times on the stage and had hurt himself by striking his head on the board. This one role alone had made him popular with the Hindus. But now everything had changed. Now people had taken to violence, generating fear and hatred. Jameel's popularity had ended with one stroke.

They walked past the wall, each vying with the other to stay in the middle and getting edged out. Ram, who was walking along the edge of the lane, saw a young man come towards them, and looked around in alarm. Barefooted, wearing a dhoti and a vest, his thick tuft flying in the air, a sandal-paste mark on his forehead, he looked a professional pundit. And, as they later learnt with the lifting of the curfew, he had hastened to this locality to conduct a pooja and was now going back home. He was looking for some co-religionist in whose company he could walk through the troubled zone.

"I'll come with you," he had said under his breath and then given a wry smile.

Grimly trying to keep close to the group, he would often get dislodged from his place and then frisk back into position with the briskness of a mouse. His antics annoyed the others, but they soon relented, thinking he was the most vulnerable of them all. His appearance would have given him away, proclaiming him to be the most Hindu among Hindus.

The narrow road looked bleak like the parting of a widow's hair. Like last night's hazy dream, Ram remembered having seen burqa-clad women walking along this road and children shrilly playing in the dust whenever he passed by this road. But they were nowhere to be seen today. Nor was old Kariman, the wood stall owner's mother whom Ram had often seen crossing the road or raucously calling out to her son, "Eh, Shabbir!" There were only some people standing before a tea-shop, scowling at passers-by without raising their heads, their lips contorted in nasty smiles.

Ram and his friends accelerated their pace, but their legs seemed to be giving in. After walking some distance they came to a Hindu basti – huts and tenements, straw roofs and garbage heaps. The drains were choked, the water in them having turned thick and black. An old man was silting in front of his house, his body caught in a paroxysm of coughing.

"I think nothing of going out alone in a dark night," the young pundit said, baring his teeth in a smile. Then he detached himself from the group and walked off, throwing out his chest. He had come to his basti.

On the main road, the two friends took a different route, leaving Ram standing there, gaping after them. Normally a busy thoroughfare, crowded with bustling people, it now lay deserted. Only a stray rickshaw or two ran past. Even the nondescript cycle repair shops which sprang up on the sidewalks every morning were missing. The other shops too were closed. Sometimes a small group of seedy-looking people would suddenly appear at one end of the road, and walking in brisk strides, as suddenly disappear round the other end. Only a few minutes back, a small batch of Muslim workers had passed by, spilling over one another like sheep. It had briefly stopped midway, looked around warily like sheep dogs and then resumed walking.

Ram walked bravely on, every once in a while looking back over his shoulder, unsure of himself like the jackal that had strayed into town. He thought there was some danger lurking in every corner, making him feel diminutive and annihilated. He seemed to be wallowing in an eerie silence in which even a small muffled voice resounded like the cry of a charging crowd. He wished he had not stirred out of his house that morning. But go to work he must. He was working in a small establishment in the Civil Lines and absence from work meant a cut in his wages.

Another small Muslim locality. People standing in small bunches in front of houses and shops glared at him as he passed them. His body went limp with fright, but he doggedly kept on for fear of running into some trouble. Then he saw a young man of about twenty, wearing a vest and lungi running towards him, brandishing a knife. Ram had, in fact, seen him from a distance and had felt so petrified that he had lost his voice and could not even shout to the P.A.C. men who had been patrolling that area and were still within hailing distance. The young man came advancing. Ram quickly stepped aside. The man ran past him laughing and disappeared into a side lane.

Ram had almost stopped breathing. He didn't even know whether he was still walking or had come to a standstill. His teeth clattered. For an instant, the faces of his wife and children revolved before his eyes.

Another man, wearing a lungi and kamiz, was heading for him. "Babuji, go your way," the man said. "There's nothing to fear. These outsiders bring a bad name to the mohalla. You look the other way for a minute and things start happening. I keep them on the leash, you know. Oh, what bad times! You buy milk from Majid, don't you?"

Ram looked at the man intently, but failed to place him. Was the fellow trying to play some trick on him?

"Yes," he answered without stopping.

"Majid is my uncle. You just walk on. There's nothing to fear. But one thing, Babuji: stay indoors for another two or three days. The times are bad. You never know. Just walk on. I'll be watching."

Ram kept walking as if in a trance. He felt that the young man was still chasing him, all the time brandishing his knife in the air.

His confidence returned as he reached the crossing. People were going about, looking lost as if they had been cut off from their moorings. Ram stood there, bewildered. Everybody seemed to be trying to escape from something. A rickshaw was coming in his direction. "Civil Lines!" the rickshawala cried. "One passenger!"

The hood of the rickshaw was leaning over to the front. So Ram could not see the other occupant of the rickshaw. He quickly settled the fare and got in. A tremor ran through his body as he settled down in his seat and looked sideways. It was a bearded Mussalman, hollow-cheeked, sunken-eyed, wearing a thin shirt and pyjamas. The man gave Ram a hostile look.

The rickshaw started. They sat there glued to the edges of their seats to keep their bodies from touching, belligerently watching each other from the comers of their eyes. Ram noticed that the man's eyes frequently travelled to his waist and his trouser pockets. Ram knew why. For that matter, he was himself keeping a watchful eye on the man's waist.

Eight or ten people were standing in a cluster on the footpath in front of an eating shop, three of them hefty, like wrestlers. One of them pointed towards the rickshaw and the others following his gaze, glared at the rickshaw.

"Ya Khuda!" the man in the rickshaw muttered. Ram looked at him startled. The man was holding his head against the hood of the rickshaw, his eyes had disappeared behind their sockets and his knees were shaking. Ram knew why the man was looking so frightened. Only a short while ago he had himself had a similar experience.

"Are you hearing me? Pull yourself up!" Ram shook the man's shoulder.

The old man gave Ram a helpless look. No sound came from his mouth.

"Are you ill?"

"No...no," the man mumbled in an indistinct voice.

"Don't get scared," Ram said, matter-of-factly. "There's nothing to get scared."

Ram was surprised at the tone of his voice. He seemed to have uttered the words mechanically, without meaning anything by them. Would he have uttered these words so blandly a few days ago, when he was still human, a feeling man?

The rickshaw had left the eating place far behind. The bearded man was now sitting straight and looking reassured. "What bad times!" he muttered.

"Yes, we are passing through very bad times," Ram echoed the old man's feelings.

"People are dying like rats. Yes, like rats in an epidemic of plague."

"Yes, both Hindus and Muslims – they are dying like rats."

"It's only the poor that get killed. I live from day to day. I earn and eat. We've gone without food for three days."

"Where do you work?" Ram asked.

"National Tailoring House," the man replied. "A grown-up can put up with hunger. But not the children. How can one bear to see one's children starving before one's own eyes? I had to come out today. There was no other way out."

"Yes, I know. That's how things are."

"Believe me, women have deserted their houses and are living in others' houses cooped up like hens. They are living in such wretched condition. I just can't explain their plight. People are starving. Some have sold their bicycles, others their watches. Some have even pawned their wives' ornaments."

"Both sides are to blame."

"I know. None is above board. I have a couple of Hindu friends. But now they avoid me. They refuse to look me straight in the face. That's god's truth. Why blame them? I also try to avoid them."

"That's the whole trouble. And one reason why we're always down and put."

"True, if we learn to live in amity, no one would dare push us around like this."

They fell silent. Their bravado seemed to have run thin. Like a sick man losing his appetite, Ram had lost his urge to talk. The rickshaw was running at a fast pace and they sat looking into the distance. Sometimes even truth can have such a false ring. Did the old man really mean it? It flashed through Ram's mind that the fellow had kept agreeing with him just to save his skin.

They had reached the Civil Lines. The bearded man asked the rickshaw- driver to stop this side of the crossing. He paid his fare and walked off without looking back. He had walked a couple of steps when he abruptly stopped as if he had remembered something. He came back to Ram and smiled as if he was going to give him some good news.

"I don't know whether I would live through the day to be able to get back home in the evening," the old man said. "Well, goodbye. God willing, we shall meet again."

He turned and swiftly walked away, throwing out his legs outlandishly. The rickshaw resumed its journey. Ram got down at the crossing.

His eyes were filled with tears. Whether they were tears of gratitude for the old man or tears of helplessness at his own plight, he could not decide. But the painful situation seemed to have given him a vicarious satisfaction. Although he was still feeling too shaken to savour any happiness or feel sad, yet his heart had softened towards the old man. The man, whom a short time ago he had taken for a murderer, was tender like a lamb. He must have been like Majid.

He looked around as he walked. Everything looked so cheerful and bright – the green trees, broad roads, beautiful shops. Then he remembered that he had to return in the evening by the same route and his heart became leaden as if a heavy weight had been placed on it. A sharp wind had risen, sounding like the moan of a woman. Or was it the groan of a child? Suddenly he heard a koel somewhere in a tree. Since the riots started, the koel must have called countless times, but he had never taken any notice of it. But now it sang on and on.

4

O, Haramzade!

Bhisham Sahni

Bhisham Sahni was born in 1915 in Rawalpindi (now in Pakistan). He was educated at Government College, Lahore, from where he took a Master's degree in English literature. After Partition in 1947, he settled down in Delhi and began to teach at a Delhi University college. He worked as a translator at the Foreign Languages Publishing House in Moscow for about seven years. On returning to India, he resumed teaching in a Delhi college. He has published various novels, collections of short stories, plays and a biography of his brother, Balraj Sahni. He also edited *Nai Kahaniyan* for some time. He won the Sahitya Akademi award for his novel *Tamas,* which has been translated into English. Many of his writings have been translated into various languages.

When caught by wanderlust, I myself do not know where I am going to land up next. It could be among ancient ruins on the shores of the Mediterranean or on the crowded street of a European city. It is indeed a strange world, puzzling and at times inaccessible. And like me, it also seems to revolve without an axis.

On one such sojourn, I happened to find myself in a remote European port-town. It was afternoon. Emerging from my hotel, I proceeded towards the bay and sat down on a bench by the edge of the sea, watching the ships coming in and going out of the harbour. A middle-aged woman who was passing by, suddenly stopped near my bench. I didn't take any particular notice of her, thinking that she might have mistaknen me for some other person. But after a moment's hesitation she approached me.

"From India?" she asked, greeting me with a faint smile.

I nodded and smiled back in reply.

'The moment I saw you, I knew you were an Indian." Depositing her shopping bag on the bench, she sat down by my side.

Evidently, she was returning after doing her morning shopping. Short and heavily built, she had blue eyes, like the water of the sea. Only children have such bright and transparently blue eyes. And her clear and flawless complexion. But I could see traces of white in her hair and lines of age on her face. From her accent I could make out that she was not from England but she had a working knowledge of English, which enabled her to communicate with me.

"My husband is also from India," she said. "He's at home and will be pleased to meet you."

One comes across a lot of Indians in England and France. Hundreds of them have settled down there permanently. But to find an Indian in that remote part of the continent – well, I was really not prepared for it. Partly out of curiosity and partly with the idea of whiling away the time, I decided to accompany her.

Walking by her side, I couldn't help looking at her roly-poly figure. What did this countryman of mine find in her to have married her and settled so far away from home? Maybe in her younger days she had been attractive and vivacious. Or, was it her blue eyes? Indians have a special fancy for fair skin and blue eyes. Now time had taken a heavy toll on her. She must be about fifty-five or so. As she walked by my side, she kept shifting her bag from one hand to the other and often lost her breath. I took the bag from her, relieving her of the burden.

"Have you been to India?" I asked.

"Yes, once. I went with Lal. But that was years ago."

"Does Mr Lal visit India often?" I asked.

The woman shook her head. "No, he hasn't been there for a long time," she said. "That's one more reason why he'll be so happy to meet you. Indians rarely come this way."

We climbed a narrow flight of stairs. There was a light burning in one of the rooms – a big room, its walls lined with almirahs, crammed with books, pictures and maps hanging from empty spaces on the walls. At the far end of the room, by the window, sat a man in a dark suit, his hair turning gray, reading a magazine.

"Lal, look who I've brought with me!" the woman said happily. "A countryman of yours."

He got up and stepped forward, curiosity writ large on his face.

"Welcome, I'm so pleased to meet you," he said, extending his hand. "They call me Lal. I'm an engineer. I'm grateful to my wife that she brought you here."

He was a tall man, rather loose-limbed, graying at the temples, though the white had also started invading other parts of the head. At the first encounter it was difficult to guess which part of the country he came from. As we sat down, he opened up with a volley of questions:

"Delhi must have changed a lot?" he asked with the eagerness of a child.

"Yes, it has," I replied. "When were you there last?"

"I don't belong to Delhi, really. I lived there in my childhood. I'm from Punjab, in fact. Jullundur, to be precise. You must have heard of Jullundur, of course?"

"I'm also from Punjab and have spent a large part of my life in Jullundur."

He got up and hugged me warmly.

"Oh, *zalim,* why didn't you tell me before?" he exclaimed. "So you've associations with Jullundur?"

I felt embarrassed. I didn't expect that an elderly man like him would get worked up in this manner. He swiftly walked into the other room and soon reappeared with his wife in tow.

"Helen, he's also from Jullundur. From my town! Why didn't you tell me before?" His face shone and the circles under his eyes became moist.

His wife who had put on an apron, gave me a smile and sat down by my side.

"I've been to India," she said. "Lal took me around the country. Agra, Banaras, Calcutta. We did a lot of travelling."

Lal was looking at me steadily, his eyes shining with the fervour typical of an Indian when he meets a native of his country. It is a love-hate relationship. An Indian first runs away from his country and then pines for it.

"Your wife told me that you've not visited India for a long time," I said. "But I'm sure that you've still some links with our country."

My eyes roved over the walls. The maps hanging from them were those of India. I looked at his wife. The memory of her visit to India seemed to have cast a shadow over her face.

"He still gets letters from Jullundur," she said. "But he won't let me read them. He shuts himself up in the room and reads those letters in privacy."

"You'll never understand." Lal's voice became thick with emotion. "I wish I could tell you what those letters mean to me."

"You roam the streets of Jullundur together," his wife said, getting up. "In the meanwhile, I'll get some tea ready for you."

I was surprised that a man could have such sentimental attachment with his country even after having lived abroad for over two decades, specially when he appeared to have broken all links with it.

"I know of another countryman of ours – a case similar to yours," I said, forcing a smile on my face. "He had not visited India for years together and pined to set foot on it and touch its soil with his own hands." I wanted to bring some comic relief into the proceedings, for it was getting too much for me. I stopped mid-way to look at his face and realised that I had erred, but I had to go on, for he was intently watching me.

"So one day he bought an air ticket for Delhi," I continued. "He got down from the plane and not caring for the rough and tumble of the airport, he bent down to touch the soil of his motherland. But as he straightened himself, his hand went to his pocket. Lo, his purse was missing!"

My host's eyes were still fixed on me. But his gaze looked so distant as if those two eyes were staring at me out of the past.

"At least your friend had the satisfaction of touching the soil," he said, dropping his voice to a whisper. "That was great!"

Then he got up abruptly. "It's an occasion!" he cried. "Our meeting together so unexpectedly. We must celebrate!"

He brought out a bottle of cognac and two wine glasses from the wine cabinet.

"You must visit India every third or fourth year," I said. 'Then you'll not feel so nostalgic."

He nodded absent-mindedly. "I went there once and then decided not to repeat my visit." The wine had set him talking. "I had run away from home, you know." He placed his hand on my knee. "I was very young at that time. That was almost forty years ago." He sat lost in thought for a while and then as if with a jolt returned to the present. "It's those small inconsequential happenings that play a decisive role in one's life," he said. "My brother had rebuked me for neglecting my studies. He said I did nothing but loaf about, wasting our father's hard-earned money.

That very night I ran away from home. I had resolved not to write home, much less come back, till I had made good in life. My mother died, waiting for me, and my father also died a few years after." A faint smile flickered around his lips and was soon extinguished.

"I went to India after about fifteen years of my playing truant from home," he said. "I had gone there with high hopes."

He was going to refill our glasses when his wife came in with tea.

"In Jullundur we lived near Mai Hiran Gate," he said picking up the threads of his narration.

"At that lime Jullundur was a modest-sized, dilapidated, faceless sort of town. Honey, do you remember where we lived in Jullundur?" He turned to his wife.

"Lal, I'm no good at remembering names," his wife said. "But I do remember the battalion of dogs that used to roam on the roads. And the drains – they stank to the skies. Our elder daughter – she was hardly two years old at that time – got scared at the sight of a housefly. She had never seen a fly before. Nor a squirrel. When she saw a squirrel jumping on to a tree…. We were staying in Lal's ancestral house."

Our talk drifted to the progress our country had made in his absence, and I found him unusually well-informed.

"You know a lot more than I do, although I live there," I said, complimenting him.

"But there's one great difference between you and me," he said. "You *live* there and I don't."

Suddenly his wife said, "Lal has not forgiven himself for marrying me."

"Helen!"

I felt embarrassed at their giving vent to their feelings in front of a stranger. 'Was India the cause of some discord between them?' I asked myself. Had they reached the threshold of old age having constant squabbles?

"I tell you, he should have married an Indian girl," she said. "Even now I keep telling him to go back to India. Our two daughters are quite grown up and can take care of themselves and I can also fend for myself." She said this in a staid, matter-of-fact manner, without any hint of complaint or malice.

"But I know he will not be happy there, either," she said after a pause. "For one thing, he won't be able to stand the heat of that place." A faint smile appeared on her face. "Besides, his links with his country have also snapped."

"Helen, please!" my host said in a pleading voice.

I learnt that they had two daughters. The elder one had followed in her father's footsteps and had qualified as an engineer. The younger daughter was still studying at the university.

They appeared to be a happy family and I thought I should not attach any importance to their emotional outbursts. These, I thought, were quirks of character which sometimes got the better of them, specially when he happened to meet one of his compatriots. I knew that when I was gone, he would again swing back into the mundane routine of his life.

"You were going to tell me about a small incident of your life," I looked up at him. His wife had gone into the kitchen.

He looked around thoughtfully, and then inclining his head to one side, smiled to himself.

"You have not lived away from your country for long," he said. "You would, therefore, not be able to appreciate the state of my mind. For the first few years, I was almost oblivious of my country as if it did not exist for me. But then I started missing it. It almost became an obsession with me. I would go out in *kurta* and *pajama* just to draw people's attention to the fact that I was an Indian. I wore *Jodhpuri chappals* which I had bought in London and felt happy when the eyes of passers-by lingered on them. I even wished that I could chew a *paan* and wear a *dhoti* just to tell them that I was not just any man in a crowd, but a somebody from India. On the Diwali night, I illuminated my house and put a *bindi* mark on Helen's forehead and red colour in the parting of her hair. But I pined for my sister on the *raksha bandhan* day. How l wished she were there to tie the sacred thiead on my wrist and say, 'Brother, may you live long and prosper.'

"That decided it. I must make a trip to India and take Helen along with our two-year old daughter. It was in my mind that if Helen found the place congenial enough, I would find a job for myself and settle down there for good.

"After visiting some places, we at last made it to Jullundur." He suddenly fell silent and started looking down. "I was sorely disappointed with my first glimpse of the city," he said, with a shrug of his shoulders. "It was still the same seedy-looking town with most of the roads in utter disrepair. Everything was familiar and yet so depressing. Nothing much had changed except the outer fringes of the town, where most of the well-to-do people now lived. Was this the town I had so eagerly brought Helen to see? The people I had known as a young boy had grown old, some of them haying shrivelled beyond recognition. My brother's face glowed as he received me, but I could see that at the back of his mind, a suspicion lurked that I had come to claim my share of the ancestral property. I would wander along the noisy streets to while away the time. I felt as if I had come to an alien city.

"One day I was passing through a bazaar when I heard someone shouting, 'O, Haramzade!' I paid no particular heed to where the call had come from. This was the traditional cat-call of our city, considered to be inoffensive enough: one heard it at all hours of the day. I was pleased. Though the city looked decayed – such being my impression after having lived in a clean city in Europe – it had kept its 'culture' alive.

"'O, Haramzade, look this way! Have you forgotten your father?'

"Yes, it was someone addressing me. Standing on the plinth of a bicycle shop, across the road, a man was excitedly waving to me.

"I looked at the man intently. Black serpentine moustache, a semi-bald head, thick glasses. Then behind those moustaches and glasses, the nebulous contours of a face gradually started taking a definite shape. Oh, it was Tilakraj, my old schoolmate!

"'Haramzade, you even refuse to recognise your father!' The next moment, we were locked in an embrace.

"'You bastard! Who do you think you are?' Tilakraj cried, his face beaming with joy. 'You think living in *vilayat* has made you a saheb? Wait, you'll know better when I poke you in your saheb's ... !'

"He had lifted me from the ground. I feared he would hurl me down on the road, so excited he looked. Then we started calling each other names, for the sheer joy of it.

"I had met one who was more than a friend of my childhood days. He had opened new vistas before me. I had staged a royal come-back to my city, to my country. Now I really belonged.

"Our antics were deliriously childish, even stupid. But they signified the moments of truth, springing straight from our hearts, whose reality I would not deny even today.

"'Come, we'll sit somewhere and have tea,' Tilakraj said, mouthing another obscenity. A punjabi friend is not a friend, unless he hurls an abuse at you, followed by a warm hug.

"Arm-in-arm, we proceeded towards Mai Hiran Gate. As of old, I was again walking the streets of Jullundur with the carefree abandon of an overlord strutting about on his *jagir.*

"'Tomorrow you're dining with me at my house,' Tilakraj announced as we came out of the eating place. 'Sala, let me see how you say 'no' to my request. I'll catch you by your throat and thrust your head into the gutter! '

"'I'll come,' I promptly replied.

'And bring your *Mem* also. I'll wait for you till eight. And if you don't come, you bastard...!'

"'As in old times, lifting his leg, he pressed it against my thigh. This used to be our parting shot. The one who did it first was supposed to have scored over the other.

"This was like make-believe. In fact, the whole trip to India was a make-believe. But some inner urge was driving me forward. I loved to be caught in this snare.

"Helen and I were at Tilakraj's house promptly at eight. I thought we would be the only guests. But the rogue had again caught me on the wrong foot. His house was swarming with guests. Perhaps he wanted to give me a big ovation.

"Tilakraj took me to the kitchen to introduce me to his wife. Her face had turned red, sitting near the hearth and some locks of hair had fallen over her forehead. Rising to her feet, she gently dabbed her hands on the end of her *dupatta* and then adjusted it over her head. A Punjabi to her core, simple, jovial, oozing with affection, her whole grace and vivacity seemed to be concentrated in that one gesture. My mother, my sister, my brother's wife – they all acted in the same manner. If you want to know what a Punjabi woman is, meet her at the threshold of her kitchen.

"'Bhabi, don't you know your husband?' I said. 'A first class idiot that he is, he has again played the fool with you. Where was the need for this formality? We had just come to meet you. It must be this mutt's doing!'

"She gave her husband an indulgent smile. 'It's no formality,' she said. 'It's the least we could do. We're lucky. Your feet have sanctified our house.'

"Words that the ladies of the house always used to welcome their guests. Words, that had been hallowed by usage through the centuries.

"She hurriedly stepped out to meet my wife. Holding her hand, she led her towards a chair and forcing her on it, sat down by her side on the floor. She knew just enough English, and, aided by gestures, she was able to make Helen understand her purport, in the end provoking a lot of mirth and laughter. She showed Helen her pieces of embroidery and when she showed interest in a Kulu shawl, she put it around her shoulders. Then she took her into the kitchen and showed her all the things she had cooked and the way the cooking had been done.

"Helen had found the proceedings rather tiring. How long can one keep up the pretence of politeness with strangers, however well-meaning one may be, especially when one has also to reckon with the barrier of language? The drinks were still on when she dumped herself into an easy chair in the verandah and catching my eye, gestured me to call it a day.

"The party came to an end around midnight and Tilakraj's friends started leaving, one by one. When we got up to go, Tilakraj almost collared me. 'So soon!' he looke dat me surprised. 'Sit down, you! Why don't you sit down? You're not going.' Bringing his robust Punjabi hospitality into full play, he forced me back into my chair.

"Wearing *salwar* and *kameez,* her hair done in a bun at the back of her neck, as Tilakraj's wife went from one room to the other, she seemed to epitomize all that is most graceful and remarkable in a Punjabi woman. Somewhere deep down in my heart, I felt with a pang, if only there had been a woman like her, flitting about in my house, singing the songs of my land – those songs which I had heard in my very young days, and the jingle of those bangles which I had not heard for many years.

"I had nothing against Helen. She had done her best to imbibe my ways. She had learnt to make chapatis, she had learnt to fry *dal* with onions. She had even picked up a few songs from me and occasionally went out for a walk with me in *salwar* and *kameez*. But now it all sounded so false – as if it was only a camouflage.

"We were about to leave when Tilakraj's wife came out rushing from the kitchen.

"'Are you going?' she asked. 'I had made mustard *saag* and maize chapatis for you!'

"I stopped. These are the two delicacies which no Punjabi can resist.

"'You should have told us before,' I said. 'We are full. There's no room for saag and maize chapatis.'

"'How could I make maize chapatis for all the guests, single-handed?' she countered. 'It takes time to make them. I've made some exclusively for you and your wife.'

"I looked at Helen. A muscle in her face twitched. 'Can't it be some other time?' she asked.

"The very mention of saag had turned me on and the drink was also doing its work.

"'Bhabi has specially cooked it for us,' I said to Helen. 'I'm sure you'll like it.'

"Without waiting for her answer, I took off my shoes. 'We'll eat in the royal Punjabi manner,' I said in a hearty voice. 'We'll squat in the kitchen and eat.'

"As Tilakraj's wife sat by the hearth baking chapatis, her earrings glinted in the glow of the fire. Red stones in gold earrings look beautiful on a Punjabi woman. She put a chapati on the iron pan. Her bangles jingled.

I was watching this most homely scene after many years. I even forgot that Helen was sitting in the drawing room, to whom

Tilakraj's wife had taken the food herself. She must have finished her food and would be waiting for me.

"When I came into the drawing-room, I found Helen sleeping in her chair. The food was lying on the table, untouched.

"It was very quiet in the lane. We hired a tonga. I hadn't had a tonga ride for ages and I thought that Helen would enjoy it. On the way she asked me how long I intended staying at Jullundur.

"'Why, are you tired of the place? I'm sorry I put you to a lot of trouble this evening.'

Helen was silent.

"'We Punjabis are mad after saag. I couldn't resist the temptation. Did you like it?'

"'Listen, how about my going back from here? You can come later when you feel like it.'

"'What are you saying, dear? Haven't you liked my people?'

"I felt I would have been happier if I had come alone. I would have gone about without any kind of constraint and it would have been a real holiday for me. But Helen had agreed to come at my insistence. I wanted her to see my native land, my people. There was a touch of asperity in Helen's otherwise mellow and calm voice. I tried to put my arm around her waist, but she pushed away my hand. I should have tried again, but I was myself feeling a bit cross.'

"The tonga ride was very jerky. It was an old, ramshackle tonga and threatened to fall apart at every step. The road was full of pot-holes and bumpy. She was doing her best to hold on to her scat.

"'I think I should go back with the child,' she repeated. 'I seem to stand in your way.'

"'You retired into your shell the moment we reached Tilakraj's house. I had brought you to meet my people.'

"'You came here to satisfy your lust, the hunger of your heart, not to show me your country,' she said in a cold voice. 'I've had enough of your country.'

"She fell silent. But as the tonga jolted forward, my anger increased. Why was she trying to get the better of me? In my anger, I didn't even see that there were tears in her eyes.

"The members of my family had gone to sleep, leaving a light burning in our room. When we were inside the room, Helen again said that I would have done well if I had married an Indian. She said it in a flat, passionless voice, as if she was discussing some insignificant detail with me. She looked at me. I felt as if her eyes were made of glass. They were cold and hard.

"'Instead, why not say that you made a mistake by marrying me – an Indian?' I said. 'Why lay the blame on me entirely?'

"'I never said anything of the sort,' she said and went behind the partition to change.

"Our daughter was sleeping in a cradle by the side of the wall. She whimpered on being disturbed in her sleep. Coming out from behind the partition, Helen tried to put her back to sleep. When the child fell asleep, she again went behind the partition.

"'It was the first time that I got an opportunity of meeting old friends, but you couldn't even stand that,' I said, peeved. 'A curse on such a marriage!'

"I knew no reply would come from behind the partition. When the child was sleeping, Helen was extra-careful not to disturb her. To talk back on an occasion like this was out of the question.

"But to my utter surprise, pat came a reply, from her: 'As if you care for me!' she said. 'You were blissfully busy in flirting with your friend's wife!'

"'Helen!' My whole body was on fire. 'What rubbish are you talking?'

I felt that with that one sentence, she had suddenly demolished something sacred, something tender and beautiful which epitomised the very culture of my country, something for which my country stood out from others. We were seeing the same thing from two worlds apart.

"'So you think I was flirting with my friend's wife?' I snarled.

"'How do I know what you were doing? But I did sense something.'

"I rushed behind the partition and slapped Helen hard oh her face. She looked at me surprised and then hid her face behind her hands. She did not cry.

"'Beat me!' she cried. 'Beat me, for all I care. I didn't know you had brought me to your country to beat me!'

"My legs shook as her words fell on my ears and my body went cold. There was a deep mark of the slap on her face. She was standing behind the partition in a chemise, with bowed head.

"'What have I done?' I kept looking at her wide-eyed. Then I went into the courtyard. But the words, 'What have I done?' kept buzzing in my ears.

"We left India three days after this incident. I had decided in my mind that I would never come here again. I bade good-bye to Jullundur forever."

I heard footsteps on the stairs and soon the door was flung open and two girls entered, laughing – Lal's daughters. Simultaneously, their mother entered the room, carrying a big plate of cakes. Turn by turn, the girls kissed their mother and father and picking up the cakes from the plate, started eating avidly.

"This gentleman is from India," Mr Lal said. "He belongs to Jullundur."

"Jullundur!" the elder girl squealed, and then greeted me with a smile. "It must have changed by now," she said. "I'm told it looked very ancient when mother visited it. No, mother?"

Mr Lal came with me to my hotel. He appeared to be an influential man of the town for I saw many passers-by raising their hats to him. I wondered which was the true face of the man – when he was pining for his country and brooding over the past, or when, as if coming from nowhere, he acted as a successful professional?

While parting, he again squeezed me between his arms. "I have no complaints," he said. "Life has been kind to me. If I have any complaint, it's only against myself."

He stood silent for a while and then smiled.

"Sometimes when I'm walking on the road, I wish that someone should call out to me, 'O, Haramzade!' and I should jump forward and hug that man!"

His voice shook as he uttered these words.

5

Not by Flesh Alone

Kamleshwar

Kamleshwar, born in 1932 in Mainpuri, Uttar Pradesh, holds a place of eminence in Hindi literature, having distinguished himself as a writer of short stories, novels and plays. He has a number of published books to his credit. He has also been associated with films. He was the first editor of the Hindi magazine, *Nai Kahaniyan,* and was also associated with the magazine *Ganga.* He was for some time the Additional Director General of Doordarshan. He passed away in 2007.

The lady doctor, after examining her, told her that though she was free from venereal disease, she had unmistakable symptoms of incipient consumption. She wrote down a long prescription for her and advised her to take nourishing diet.

The Municipal Committee had put a ban on indiscriminate prostitution. Those who failed in the medical test were worried. They had been asked to fold up their business and did not know how to fend for themselves. The lucky few, who came through in the test, strutted about saucily, bragging about their high pedigree. The comely ones, whom Ibrahim, the Contractor, had taken under his wing, infiltrated into decent localities of the city. The fellow kept an eye on them, and paid them month by month, at contracted rates, keeping the rest of their earnings for himself.

At her wits' end, Jugnu also approached Ibrahim to find her a place somewhere. "Do you think it's that simple?" Ibrahim said curtly, "It's easier to palm off a girl to a bridegroom than to find a place for her. Customers are choosy. They prod and probe each tissue of a girl's body." Then he edged past her hautily.

His remarks came as a blow to Jugnu. She thought she was still good for many years. The second blow, however, settled it. Shahnaz, the girl in the next balcony waved her hands in the air and said, "Arre, don't put on airs. The day is soon coming when no one will climb the stairs to your balcony."

The whole lane was scandalised at Shahnaz's ominous prophecy. No one ever fulminated like this even at one's worst enemies. May the visitors have strength in their loins and more money in their pockets.

That evening, Fatte came to her with a new man. The man lingered at the door, as if not sure of himself. In khaki trousers and a blue shirt, there was a stubble on his chin and he carried a bag in one hand. Jugnu's searching eyes detected a thin film of dust on his eyebrows and earlobes. She moved away from him and sat down on her cot. But the man kept standing, clutching the bag. She quietly took away the bag from him and put it by the side of the pillow.

But the man still showed no signs of moving. "Take off your shoes," she said impatiently.

When the man removed his shoes, a wave of stench rose from his feet, filling the small room. Many others who visited her stank the same way when they peeled off their clothes; specially, Mansu, the grocer, who invariably came to her after eleven. When he had finished, he would sit there holding the small of his back, as if he was stone dead. Jugnu had to help him to his feet and he would totter out of the room, scratching his thigh. For that matter, Kanwarjeet, the hotel-keeper, smelled no less and he kept belching loudly, uttering 'au', 'au' with every belch.

When Jugnu could not stand the smell of the man's feet, she asked him to put on his shoes.

He obeyed without demur and then sat stock still on the edge of the cot. Jugnu was annoyed. "Do you think you are sitting in your father's drawing room?" she said testily. "Unload yourself and bump off!"

The man felt slighted but he soon regained his composure. "What's your name?" he asked in a faltering voice.

"Jugnu."

"Where do you come from?"

"How does it concern you where I come from?" she said peeved. "Let's get down to business."

Then like every other person he asked: "Do you like your profession?"

"Yes, don't you?"

She stretched herself on the cot and pulled up her sari, baring a part of her thighs. He also lay down by her side and his hand moved up to her blouse.

"Don't be a pest," she said, hastily pushing away his hand. "Keep your hands off my blouse."

Completely put out, the man lay still by her side and looked at her face. There was a coating of cheap powder on her face, and lines of powder, like white strings, round her neck. Her lips were blotchy, as if blood clung to them in clots and her ear tops stood out like the eyes of a frog. Her hair was smeared with oil. The pillow case was soiled and the bed sheet looked like a crumpled jasmine flower.

Then his eyes roved over the room. In one comer lay a pitcher of water with an enamel mug by its side. There were some rags also in the same comer. By the side of the cot stood a small cupboard, in which lay a broken comb, a cheap nail polish and some hair pins. A few names and addresses were scribbled in pencil on one side of the cupboard, in another comer lay some film song books in a small heap and by their side some tasselled pigtails like coiled serpents. The man's mind was filled with revulsion. To take his mind off what he saw around him, he put his hand on Jugnu's thigh. The flesh was rubbery like stale fish and rough like coarse cloth. From her semi-exposed body rose a faint smell of starch.

"You may have all the time in the world, but not me," she said at last. "This is my hour of business. By now I would have ticked off four men." She firmly clutched the man in her arms.

When he got up from the cot, Jugnu, as if in jest, opened his bag. "You seem to carry a lot of money in the bag," she laughed. The man thought she wanted to filch another rupee or two. But the bag contained only a sheaf of loose papers, a newspaper and a loaf of bread.

"Don't forget me, when you visit the lane next time," she said as the man made for the door. "Come up straight to me." The man turned round, and for the first time, closely looked to her.

Whenever Jugnu went out, she covered her head properly like a respectable woman. She did not do anything that invited lascivious remarks. They just cast longing looks at her, as all lustful men do, and no more. As she walked, she would look at them from the comer of her eye, specially at those who had visited her and seemed to have a right over her. Then one day she saw him – the man with the bag. He was standing in the verandah of the first storey of a building, smoking a *bidi*, his elbows resting on the railing. He was wearing the same blue shirt. The shadow of a flag flying over the building trembled over his shoulder.

She stopped under the building to have her *chappal* mended. She didn't look up, but she knew the man had gone inside his room.

He came to her again that night. There was a hint of recognition in his eyes. This time he did not linger at the door but came in and sat down on the cot.

"What sort of job do you do?" she asked him.

"Nothing much," he replied. "I work among labourers."

"We are also labourers," she smiled. "You must take care of us also."

"Aren't you ready yet?"

"I'm not well today," she said in a listless voice.

"What's wrong?"

'I have a backache and my body seems to be going to pieces. I don't know what's gone wrong with me. May I call Tara? She's a nice girl. You'll like her."

He shook his head and after a while rose to go. "I dropped in just to see you," he said. Then he climbed down the dark stairs and was gone.

Jugnu came out and stood at the window. There were not many people in, the lane. A few stragglers stood about in small groups. A man broke away from the group every now and then and climbed up a staircase. Smoke curled up from the chimney of the baker's shop. She looked up at the wreath of the curling smoke, thinking all the while that the man would have gone to some other girl. Then she saw him slowly walking through the lane. So he had not gone elsewhere. The thought pleased Jugnu. Turning back from the window, she closed the door and lay down on her cot.

The room was damp and a nondescript bottled-up smell seemed to pervade it. Jugnu picked up a book of film songs and started reading it.

There was a knock at the door and then Amma's voice, "Jugnu, my pet, you have been in a long time. I hope the wretch has not passed out."

"There's no one with me, Amma."

"Then come out on the balcony, child. There's a fine breeze blowing. The lane is full of people." Amma flung open the door. "Are you unwell?" she asked, as she saw Jugnu lying on the cot.

"Yes, Amma. I'm feeling out of sorts. There seems to be something wrong with me."

"Better have a cup of milk, child," Amma said. "There's still time. Someone may yet turn up."

As Jugnu rose from her bed, Amma held her neck with the back of her hand to make sure that she was not running a temperature and then she noticed the fold of flesh round her waist. "Your waist is getting thick," she said. "Don't neglect your morning exercise."

Suddenly there was sound of squabbling in another comer of the building, "Lo, that witch is at it again!" Amma said, alarmed. "She'll not allow herself to be saddled without creating a fuss. I tell you, some day there's going to be a murder in her room."

It was an everyday occurrence. Bilquis complained that Amma blamed her for nothing, for she was a spirited girl and no one left her room without having his back twisted. She said she was made that way and got huge fun out of it. When a man was about to depart, she would plant herself at the door and jeer at him. "Eh, Zubeda, darling," she would call her friend, "look at this Rustam – the he-man!" she would say clapping her hands. "The wretch can't even make love properly."

One day a man flared up at Bilquis' riotous behaviour. "Stop barking, you bitch!" he exclaimed.

"Begone, you offspring of a water carrier!" Bilquis retorted. "Here, take this four-anna bit. Buy some *malai* to build up your vitality!"

Utterly crestfallen, the man quietly descended the stairs, without looking back. The fact was that all the inmates of the building were scared of Bilquis. They feared that one day she may do something ghastly. That she was not the one to be tamed easily. "I can even crush a he-man between my thighs," she would say, gesticulating boastfully.

She missed no opportunity to taunt Jugnu. "You're done for," she would tell Jugnu. "Go and find a permanent 'perch' somewhere like a domesticated animal." Jugnu did not mind. She knew Bilquis was foul-mouthed and did not even spare Amma, who took care of all the girls. "You're spreading like a buffalo," Amma would warn a girl and advise her to wear a satin petticoat. She would tell another to consume less tea and a third to cut out potatoes. She had only one worry: "If I could, I would never let you girls grow old," she would say wistfully.

Jugnu came out into the balcony and watched the passersby. The crowd was gradually thinning out and the flower sellers were closing their shops. Mannan, the gardener, as he passed by, flung a garland in Kalawati's window, and Kalawati as usual, made an obscene joke and then grinned at him. Then Jugnu saw Banne, the whitewasher, making straight for Shahnaz's staircase.

Chunnilal, who was slightly loony, had already spread his mat in front of Shanker the betel seller's shop and was singing lustily. "I'll chop off my hand if anyone can detect a false note in my singing," he declared."O, cruel one," he sang on, "You'll be drawn towards me of your own accord. O, cruel one, we'll have our honeymoon on this mat. O, cruel one...!"

Jugnu suddenly saw the man in the blue shirt at the turning of the lane. Perhaps he had returned to town and had gone to someone else. She watched closely. But no, it was not the man in the blue shirt. Her mind had been playing tricks with her.

He visited her again after a gap of many days. Coming into her room, he lay down on the cot as if it was his own house. He did not take off his shoes.

"May I know your name?" Jugnu said lying down by his side.

"Madanlal...why?"

"I just wanted to know your name. I'm seeing you after a long time."

"I couldn't come. I was in jail. There was a spate of arrests. I was one of them."

"What happened?"

"There was a strike on. The mill owners had me put behind the bars. I had a hard time getting out."

"Do these strikes bring any results? Why did they go on strike?"

"Some workers were arbitrarily retrenched – that is, without proper notice. Anyway, you won't understand these things. There were other reasons, besides. May I take off my shoes?"

"You may, if you like."

The room was filled with the stench from his canvas shoes and perspiring feet. Jugnu was not upset. She had got accustomed to the smell. In fact, it seemed to have seeped into her mind and become a part of her being.

It was in those days that the prostitutes were called up and asked to submit to medical examination. The lady doctor had told Jugnu that she had no venereal disease, but there were unmistakable signs of consumption. And then she had started coughing and running a temperature. Amma had taken her to the hospital but her temperature did not show any sign of coming down. Gradually, she became useless for nightly exertions. One day she spat blood. "Throw her out!" Bilquis fumed. "This wretch will infect all of us." Amma, of course, asked the girl to shut up, but she was herself deeply concerned at Jugnu's condition. She advised her to go away somewhere for a change and also promised to give her some money to tide over her lean days.

With all doors closed upon her, Jugnu at last sought admission in a sanatorium. In between, she came to see Amma for a day or two. "Child, don't tell them that you are living in a sanatorium," Amma advised her. "Tell them that you are staying with a sister at Rampur. The Police Inspector made my life a hell in your absence. He suspects you arc secretly plying your business in some lodgings."

Amma was pained to see Jugnu's miserable condition. Her hair had started thinning and her complexion had become blotchy.

Despite the restrictions on prostitution, many new girls had come from Lucknow and Banaras and had completely spoiled the market. She was told that Shahnaz had lost her old glory and

Kalawati could scrape just enough to keep going. Before going away, Jugnu asked for a small loan from Amma. But Amma said she was herself in strained circumstances and had no money to spare. Jugnu had every reason to feel worried.

As she passed through the lane, she cast wistful glances at those who used to visit her in the first bloom of her youth.

Mansu, the grocer, was sitting in his shop. She recalled how he would squirm, holding his back and then go away scratching his thigh. Kanwarjeet, the hotel owner, was also there, in his soiled, crumpled pyjamas, busy counting the money. The way he belched before getting out of her cot would make her feel queasy.

She could not stay in the sanatorium for long. She knew that one day she would have to return to her trade. But she was grateful to those who had not turned their backs on her in her days of need. Whatever money they had given her, she had carefully written down on the back of her prescription. Kanwarjeet after much ado had given her a loan of forty-seven rupees. Mansu had been less pretentious, but he had thrown a broad hint that she should soon return the money as if a sum of twenty-five rupees was going to give a serious setback to his business. Sant Ram, the fitter, had made a lewd joke while giving her twenty rupees. "One night in lieu of interest – agreed?" Jugnu was incensed. But she felt reassured. Her body was still good enough to sustain people's interest. That was indeed some consolation.

When hard-up, she had taken a loan of thirty rupees from Madanlal too. "I'm giving it from the party fund," he said. "Return the money as soon as you can." She knew that he was a man of limited means. But his request had a ring of sincerity. "Please don't take me amiss," he added and then went away to his party office.

She was heavily under debt and to make matters worse, the police harassed her to pay up their monthly quotas, which had been in arrears for the past seven months. They looked askance at any lapse in this matter.

Since her return from the sanatorium, she had been feeling very weak and found it difficult to put up with the night's strain. Even a little patting and cuddling brought a fit of coughing and she would start panting after a few minutes. And those people – they just threw their full weight on her chest. She bought an old pigtail from Kalawati and had also started using cups over her bosom. Taking them off and putting them on once every while was a messy affair. But she had to do it. Much to her discomfort, she also wore fully starched saris, for they made her body look filled out.

But despite all this care, her income was fast dwindling. Not many people turned up at night, and many a night she drew a blank and would just lie in bed moaning over her precarious existence, her broken body.

The sexually incompetents were the worst of the lot. They made up for their incompetence by playing with her body without coming to the point. She resented them for she found them too demanding. Better than them were those who came like loaded guns and then went their way without creating any fuss.

Every day she was sinking deeper into the mire. But there was no way out for she never had sufficient money to pay off her debts.

She was going to the barber-surgeon to consult him about the abscess on her thigh-joint when Mansu waylaid her. "It's a long time now," he said. "You're having a roaring business. What about my money?" They stepped aside from the road.

"Believe me, I don't save a paisa," Jugnu said apologetically. "I'm having a hard time of it. A pity, you've stopped visiting me."

"I've stopped going to women," Mansu said blandly. "I've taken an oath on the holy Ganga water not to touch women. Look, I now wear a rosary of tulsi beads round my neck."

Jugnu could not help smiling and Mansu looked at her, discomfited.

They resumed their walk. Owing to the abscess, Jugnu walked with a lurch. Mansu looked greedily at her staying hips. "Well, you haven't told me when you'll return my money," he asked again as they came to the end of the lane.

"Pick your money off my body if you have the strength," Jugnu said coquettishly, and then felt embarrassed at her own remark. But why maintain a false facade of dignity? She didn't want to die with a debt on her conscience.

The barber-surgeon told her that it would take time before the abscess was ripe enough for an incision and gave her a poultice to apply on the thigh. When she returned, it was getting on to be afternoon. Her coprofessionals were sitting in front of their rooms, holding a gossip-session, as a prelude to their preparations for the night's business. A group of teenagers passed through the lane, cutting lewd jokes at the women. One of the pimps chased them away. But they stopped at the end of the lane, and lifting their legs, they pulled up their dhotis or pyjamas, made obscene gestures at the women and then bolted.

As the evening approached, the lane became alive. The flower sellers loudly hawked their garlands and the paan shops glittered with lights. A policeman came and settled down in front of Gaffoor's shop. This was a cue for Gaffoor to bring out bottles of liquor and sell them openly to the night revellers.

In the evening, Jugnu removed the poultice from her thigh, and after sprucing herself, moved onto the balcony. The abscess had formed into a hard knot and gave her much pain. But in spite of that, she managed to handle a customer or two. As she sat in the balcony, she often wondered what lay in store for her. Would she have to go through life like a lame mare? Or would she be reduced to a state of penury, and like Bibbo and Champa, be driven to wearing a *burqa* and begging for alms in the name of Allah, outside the mosque? In moments of extreme dejection, she even thought of taking poison or jumping into a well.

Hundreds had come and gone, but she saw none among them who would have given her refuge. Those from whom she had borrowed money were closely known to her. But she could not rely on them either. With age the fire of passion cooled down. They became staid, raised families and took to other pastimes. Gone were the old familiar faces. To live in the past had become a torture.

The only silver lining in a dark cloud was her creditors who had not forgotten her. They often came to her to get their money's worth. She knew Mansu would come again and true to her expectation, come he did.

He still stank in the same way and as usual came after eleven. Due to the pressure on her thigh, she cried out in pain. All strength seemed to have drained from her body. She could not even take him up to the door so that he should go away scartching his thigh.

When the stiffness in Mansu's back let up a little, he sat up in the cot. "I hope you're keeping the count," he said.

"Yes," Jugnu replied, helping him out of the bed.

The night was far advanced. Jugnu lay in bed staring at the wall, though there was nothing to see – except dirty, brown patches where she had once pasted up photographs of film stars cut out from film magazines. On a nail in a comer dangled a bunch of old glass bangles on a string, and in another corner along the wall lay an empty vial of nail polish.

Under the cot lay a small bundle of old tattered clothes and a tin box which, among other things, contained a piece of paper, its letters completely faded and indistinct. It was a dead letter having no meaning for her. She was past caring, for now there was no one to call her back. Between his life and hers, the river of time had flowed past, cutting through the banks till she and her man were flung apart. When she got up in the morning, her body seemed to be falling part. The pain in her thigh had increased and she had again put on the poultice. But by evening, she was again ready to face the night's ordeal. Going back to her room, she looked through the account, which she had scribbled on the side of the cupboard, showing her who had been to her how many times and how much amount still remained to be liquidated.

For his twenty rupees, Sant Ram, the fitter, who was the most brazenfaced of the whole lot of her visitors, had already been to her four times and when he was about to go away after his fifth visit, Jugnu said, "What about the payment?"

"What payment?" Sant Ram's eyebrows went up.

"I squared up your account last time," Jugnu said in an abject manner.

"One helping is permissible in lieu of interest," Sant Ram winked at her. "Surely, you don't expect payment for nothing."

Jugnu looked at him, distraught. It was not in her nature to squabble like the other girls.

Kanwarjeet, the hotel keeper, was her biggest creditor. He had visited her only thrice, which meant that her debt had diminished by fifteen rupees. She had also reduced Mansu's debt to the extent of twenty rupees. She was still savouring the happy thought when the pain in her thigh aggravated. And then there was a knock at the door. It was Madanlal. His untimely visit galled her, as if he was a loan shark come to demand his money. But even so, she called him in. He put down his bag by the pillow and sat down on the cot. Jugnu looked inside the bag. There were a few posters, a flag neatly folded in two and two musty, dog-eared registers. Her heartbeat increased. She feared that he may ask her to pay up his debt.

"You've come after a long time," Jugnu said, breaking the silence.

"May I take off my shoes?"

"Yes, you may."

"May I close the door?"

"I'm in much pain. I've an abscess on the joint of my thigh. I can lie on my back but if I bend my knees, the pain shoots up, unbearably." Madanlal suddenly stopped unlacing his shoes and looked at her, embarrassed. Jugnu was feeling none too well, but his presence seemed to have cheered her up.

After chatting with her for a while Madanlal rose from the cot "I'll go now," he said picking up his bag. Then he cast a hungry look at her – as if he was reluctant to go.

"Your money...." Jugnu said in a faltering voice.

"No, no, I didn't come for the money," he said. "I came for you."

The sweat under his armpits shone like blobs of black ink and the veins on his forearms stood out. With his sweaty hand he caught Jugnu's hand. His hand was limp and warm like a fresh loaf of bread.

"I'll come some other time," he said and was gone.

Jugnu came out into the balcony. She was sorry that she had to turn him away, disappointed. From the balcony she kept looking at his receding figure till he stopped in front of the fourth house from hers. It gave her heart a wrench to find him standing there. Then she saw him disappearing into the stairs of that house. Her abscess suddenly throbbed with pain and she winced. Then the pain slowly subsided. Had she asked him, he would have perhaps agreed to stay back. She knew he had gone away, realising the wretched state she was in. There was no trickery in his sweaty hand.

Then Kanwarjeet appeared at the door – like an intruder. Despite her rising hatred, she gave him a pale smile and led him into her room. Kanwarjeet closed the door and put up the latch.

"Today I'm in much pain," Jugnu said in a listless voice. "The abscess may burst any time."

"It hasn't healed up yet?" he asked.

"It may still take a day or two," Jugnu said in an apologetic tone clearly suggesting that he should stop pestering her.

"I'll do it very smoothly," Kanwarjeet said lying down in the cot.

"But today..."

Without allowing her to complete her sentence, Kanwarjeet held her hand and gently pulled her down on the cot. Turning on her side Jugnu switched off the light.

Suppressing her groans, she tried to shake off Kanwarjeet. Dark shadows descended before her eyes and as his weight fell upon her, she felt as if her thigh would tear apart. Kanwarjeet hesitated once or twice and then the demon seemed to have possessed him.

"It'll be over in a minute," he said in a voice loaded with passion and then firmly clutched her body.

"You're killing me," she cried, fluttering like a wounded bird. She struggled for a while and then fainted.

"Sali!" Kanwarjeet fumed, and letting go of her, sat up by her side.

After a few minutes, when Jugnu came to, she waited for the pain to subside. Then she took a piece of cloth from under the cot and switched on the light. Her whole thigh was covered with pus. Kanwarjeet was sitting a little apart from her, looking very stupid, and belching every now and then.

"It has burst, has it?" he said getting up from the cot. Jugnu covered her thigh with her sari.

"Keep a note of the count," he said moving towards the door. "It makes four times." Then he opened the door and slipped out of the room. Pulling off her sari Jugnu started cleaning up the pus. The sight of so much pus sent tremors through her heart and she called for Fatte in a feeble voice. When Fatte came, she asked him to bring her some water from the pitcher. She dipped a rag in the water and started wiping off the pus from her thigh.

"Listen, Fatte," she said while cleaning her wound. "A short while ago a man climbed up Bimla's stairs. If he is still there, ask him to see me before he goes away. He's wearing a blue shirt and carries a bag."

"A customer?" Fatte asked.

"No, a friend. And please give me some more water."

When Fatte brought her the water she said, "Forget about it. You need not call that man. He said he would come some other time."

She pressed the abscess. Some more pus came out. She winced and sweat broke out on her face.

6

Miniature Tajmahals

Rajendra Yadav

Rajendra Yadav was born at Agra in 1929 and graduated from Agra College in 1951. An outstanding figure in contemporary Hindi literature, he was responsible for introducing modern sensibility in Hindi through original works comprising a dozen collections of short stories and seven novels, one of which, *Sara Akash,* has been made into a 'new wave' film. He has also published a book of poems, an anthology of Hindi short stories and a book of literary criticism besides translations of Chekhov and Camus into Hindi. He is associated with a publishing house as its Managing Director and is the editor of *Hans.*

Meera did not broach it, nor did he. But they had realized the piquancy of the situation before they met and knew that somehow they must get out of it. But they temporised. Many times he came desperately close to the point of asking Meera if their relationship could not take a permanent form. But he was afraid that, as before, she may take it amiss. Now they felt constrained, each poised for the other's gambit.

He did not quite know why, but the beauty of the Taj had always left him cold. In fact, the glare of the white marble hurt his eyes and he sat with his back towards it. Maybe the glare was equally painful to Meera, but she seemed to like it, none the less. Perhaps there were shady patches somewhere towards the Jamuna, but here under the naked sun, one was only conscious of the intolerable glinting mass of marble.

Meeting after three years, they had diffidently smiled at each other. "Well, here we are again, the same as before." Meera, however, looked more chic. As for him – perhaps it made no difference how he looked. He remembered the innumerable monologues and catechisms of love he had with himself while sitting with her. He had seen visions of his love being requited. And now, here they were together, awkwardly greeting each other with a smile. From the very beginning, he had sensed the futility of this meeting. They had nothing new to talk about anyway, having repeatedly ranged over the entire gamut of topics to the point of staleness.

Meera was now sitting before him, her knees pulled up, one hand resting quietly on the grass. Only her fingers drummed mechanically, as if beating time to the faint echoes of a distant melody. On one finger she wore an iron ring – perhaps to counter the influence of Saturn. He reached out and squeezed her hand between his palms. The flood-gates of talk opened.

A tiny insect with a long antennae-like proboscis crawled down her neck. Vijay watched undecided and then looked away. The steps leading to the gateway were obscured by the bushes and the archway looked as if suspended in air. When his gaze travelled back, the insect was comfortably ensconced near her breast. He flicked it away. Unmindful, Meera was busy describing with gusto the assortment of guests who had come to her friend's wedding party. Warily looking around, Vijay pulled her to him. She did not resist. Her lips trembled and then shadowy lines of a faint frown appeared on her face and gently rippled into a smile, tantalizing, like the interplay of light and shade. Overwhelmed, he bent to remove her glasses for fear of their getting broken. And there it was – rising behind the fountain, like trim sycamores, the images of two Taj Mahals imprinted on her smoked glasses – two delicate toys cunningly carved in milk-white ivory.

He did not know why, but he had never liked the Taj. It always stood behind him, like an aged sentinel mounting guard. Like a foreign particle lodged between the teeth, irritant to the tongue. The Taj, even when he was absorbed in talk, impinged itself upon his attention – a massive structure, which he had never succeeded in visualizing in its integrated wholeness. He thought he would sometimes fly over the Taj and see it as a bird does. He had seen an odd photograph or two, which made the Taj more likeable. But he could not bear these sun-baked

Taj Mahals reflected in her glasses. His ebullience suddenly subsided. With a faint sigh, he pulled away his hands.

Embarrassed, Meera looked around. No one was about. Only a few persons, apparently work-hands, ran on the nearby red rampart, joking and chasing one another like monkeys on a spree. Meera smoothed her sari at the sides, put on her glasses and looked at her watch. Vijay had plucked a thistle-flower and holding it by the stem was revolving it restively.

The silence was becoming oppressive. Vijay thought that unless one of them broke the ice, something dear to both of them would get crushed under the weight of their silence.

"It's late. Shall we make a move?" he asked, idly making geometrical patterns on his palm with the flower stem.

Meera nodded. They were silent for some time, neither making a move. Then Vijay listlessly tied his shoe laces, swept aside the orange peels and groundnut shells from the newspaper and collected their things. They rose and proceeded towards the gate.

Vijay guessed it must be three – it was too much of an effort to consult his watch. The sun blazed and he wiped the sweat from his neck. They had come at noon. What an odd time for a tryst! It had made him laugh. Coming ahead of time, he had waited for her and as time passed, his impatience increased. Was his watch slow? He waited and still no sign of her. These girls, how annoying they could be. He sat with his back to the entrance, hoping that when he suddenly turned his head, lo, she would be there. He looked back a couple of times, but the magic did not work. He had not seen her for three years and he started speculating as to what

Meera would look like, what dress she would be wearing, and how she would greet him. Would she cling to him in a frenzy of love? No, it was too much to expect. Such things had never happened with him. One never knew, though.

When at last she appeared in the distance, he kept his eyes on her approaching figure. He tried, ineffectually, to take his eyes off her, to simulate the thrill of a chance encounter. But when she was with him, he could say nothing beyond a laconic, "Namaste, Meeraji."

Meera smiled, a little abashed. They sat down in the lawn in a matter of fact way, as if they had been meeting almost every day.

"I thought you would never come – that you had forgotten."

"Your letter was there to remind me. I thought the time a little odd though."

"Yes, it's not a full-moon winter night." He realized the crudity of his joke and added a little seriously, "But we have everything to ourselves at this hour." He mentally repeated the words to himself. Two persons in love and the scorching heat of noon. Was it really love?

The hour was indeed odd. The glare of the white marble was blinding. A curse seemed to have fallen on them which had cooled off the passion of their love. Were they in love, or had something changed in them? He could see no change except that Meera's complexion had improved.

Even while returning, he could not understand what had made the situation so burdensome... Walking on the gravel pathway, they would slowly reach the stairs. Defying the bold, greedy looks of the guides and the gatekeepers, they would pass through the gateway, take a rickshaw or a tonga, and as they reached the first turning, the whole thing would vanish. The next day he would write: "Meera, my behaviour yesterday might have amazed you. It might have even caused you pain. But ..." Then he saw the projection of the Taj in her glasses. "Two Taj Mahals floating upon your eyes ...." What an ingenious construction, like a line of new fangled poetry. Had Tagore seen it, he would not have written: "A teardrop on the face of Time." He would instead have said, "The silvery fish-shaped image of the Taj reflected in the tear throbbing on the cheek." But he had seen no tears in Meera's eyes; they were stone-dry.

And he would write in the letter: "I am not echoing Huxley. Somehow the Taj never held any fascination for me. But when for the first time I saw it reflected in your eyelids, I was completely taken aback. That moment I was reminded of a strange incident...."

Oh yes, now he could recall why he had suddenly become sad. "It was merely a passing incident for me...." He would write. The person whom he was mentally addressing, he thought, was not the Meera who was walking by his side. She was quite another Meera – the denizen of his mind. It was really the attraction of that Meera, the idol of his imagination, that drew him to this mundane Meera. There were many things which he did not quite like in this mundane Meera, who was walking beside him. For instance... He tried to recall Meera's odd habits which had jarred on him. For instance, why did she sidestep on to the grass and not walk straight on the gravel path?

They pursued their own thoughts as they walked side by side, anxious at the same time to catch each other's words. But no one spoke. He could not help smiling to himself as a thought flitted across his mind: when they would be getting old – say in their forties – they would ruminate over the follies of their youth and chuckle over their secret rendezvous at the Taj.

"It must have been a couple of years ago..." the undercurrents of his thoughts kept on shaping a letter. He wouldn't write all this in the letter, of course. He was merely trying to arrange, in a coherent sequence, the memory of an event which had occurred a few years ago.... He, Dev, Rakaji and Munmun were returning from the Taj in the same way as they were returning today, quiet, sad, lost. It was evening and the shadows had lengthened.

He remembered it clearly. It was the month of September. Returning from college, he had just sat down to tea when he was told that he was wanted outside.

He got up in a huff.

"You here?"

"Do you recognize me?"

"Not recognize *you*?"

But the fact was that he had not been able to place the visitor. He had, of course, met him somewhere, perhaps in Calcutta. Memory often plays tricks. He simulated recognition hoping that their talk would give him a clue to the man's identity. "Please do come in."

"No, Mr Mathur. My wife and child are waiting at the end of the lane." He apologized for the intrusion.

"But why not call them in?"

"Well, you see, we came to visit the Taj. We thought we would look you up. We did not know your place and it took some finding. Are you very busy? You see, the thing is, we must go back today."

He was standing with one foot on the steps. "Oh, no formality. Slip into your shoes and we'll be off."

Their car was at the end of the lane. The rear door of the car was open and a woman was reclining against the mudguard. She was wearing a deep green Bangalore silk sari, her coiffure was a Bengali bun with a brilliant octagonal star stuck into it. One arm was around a child of five, holding him back from sliding down the boot of the car, and with the other she guided his finger in tracing the letter T-A-J on the dusty mudguard.

She smiled in greeting and said, "You remember we promised..."

"But this lordship here was reluctant to join us," the man interrupted, and added: "Raka, please get in. If it gets dark, we will miss all the charm."

Raka ... Raka ... well, the name had a familiar ring.

"You remember, of course, the first time we met in Calcutta. We had detained you till late in the night." He looked at her. Fair complexion, round earrings, lips lightly touched, her elbows resting on the window of the car to keep the sari from fluttering in the breeze.

Yes, now he recalled. They had met in a New Market restaurant when he was on a visit to Calcutta. And afterwards they had invited him to their Lower Circular Road flat where he had dinner, followed by music. Raka played on the sitar. Mr Dev worked in a British firm and preferred western music, particularly symphonies. He took out some long playing records with beautiful plastic covers, and several times brought up the name of Tchaikovsky (or some name ending in 'ovsky'), whose records, he said, had cost him over fifty rupees each. In between, Mr Dev told him that they would love to visit Agra and see the Taj. "I visited it a long time ago in my childhood," he said. "The impression that lingers in niy mind may not tally with the present-day city. After our marriage we had decided that we would visit the city once at least. We'll have a good time, now that you live in Agra."

After dinner, they took Vijay to his place at Vivekananda Road. On the way, the snatches of talk, the echoes of the sitar and the trembling wail of the symphony kept haunting him. It made him happy to think of this contented couple. The child came later. They had named him Munmun.

Vijay wondered what Mr Dev's full name could be. How should he find out? His eagerness became obsessive. "You have a wonderful memory," Vijay said.

"Your name always came up whenever we talked of the Taj, and we talked of it almost every other day." Mr Dev looked at Rakaji. "Today is the seventh anniversary of our wedding. Munmun was not born when you visited us."

"Munmun, you have not wished your uncle," Raka said, and made the child fold his hands in respect. "He's a terror. I have to keep an eye on him all the time."

"Congratulations!" Vijay said looking at Mr Dev and Raka. But he sensed they were withdrawn from each other and a chill air hung between them.

"I hope you are well," Vijay could not help asking Raka.

She straightened a hair clip and smiled. "Perhaps it's the journey," she said. "We were in the car for five hours."

They took a long time doing the Taj. Munmun walked between Mr Dev and Raka, holding their hands. Sometimes they got so absorbed in themselves, Vijay felt like an intruder. Then Mr Dev started playing with Munmun, rolling a coin on the black and white inlaid marble floor and chasing it with the child. Rakaji was with Vijay, absorbed in studying the trellis-work, the floral engravings and passages from the Quran etched on the doors.

The evening had turned golden under the declining sun; the opaque green of the lawn had mellowed into softness, and the brooding leaves of the palms waved in the breeze; looking like pigeons gambolling with outstretched wings, ready to scatter flame-red flowers.

They moved into the vault. They shouted one another's names. Their voices echoed and re-echoed and shivering like gossamer floated into the unknown. Mr Dev kept at it for a long time, as if something deep within him was finding release on the crest of the vibrating sounds. Again and again he shouted Munmun's and Raka's names and then intently listened to the echoes as if he would have clutched them in his hands if he knew how. When he succeeded in wrenching himself away from the vault and came up, he looked tired and dejected. Taking Munmun from Vijay, he pressed him to his heart.

Rakaji was standing by the turret near the river, gazing at the railway bridge and the city beyond. The reflection of gray clouds in the vermilion sky was spread over the river like a colour wash. Raka's sari clung to her body and a lock of her hair fluttered in the breeze. Standing alone, she was, perhaps, thinking of Mumtaz Mahal and wondering if they would raise a similar mausoleum in her memory. Or, perhaps her mind was a blank. The very atmosphere of the place was such, Vijay mused; it evoked melancholy feelings.

Munmun standing behind a low wall was looking down at the river and waving at the passing children. With his elbows resting on the wall, Vijay stood by him, gazing at the current and at the thick rows of trees. At a distance from them Rakaji was still standing near the turret, her head bent, holding her fluttering sari. Mr Dev had stolen by Vijay's side. He stood there brooding.

"You have a queer feeling when you hear these sounds in the vault, don't you?" he said. "It's like calling a loved one lost in a deserted mountain forest. You shout, and the sound does not come back, nor does the loved one. But the sound keeps on reverberating and then dissipating in space still persists in its calling. You feel as if the wandering soul of the loved one has been calling since eternity and then getting dissolved in these echoes helplessly bobs up and down on its vibrations, unable to take human shape."

The distorted image of the Taj shivered into pieces in the swirling water. In spite of himself Dev's eyes brimmed with tears.

One can't feel otherwise in a melancholy place like this, Vijay thought. "When one loves, and loves dearly, and finds himself in such a gloomy atmosphere, he is likely to feel depressed," Vijay said, trying to cheer up Dev. "Let's go to the lawn. A little game with Munmun and you will feel better."

Dev took a deep sigh and looked at Vijay unhappily.

"Do you know, Mr Vijay...?" He placed his hand on Vijay's shoulder. His lips trembled. Vijay looked up, surprised at the tone of Dev's voice.

"Yes?"

They saw a green sari fluttering above them, and they descended the steps in silence.

"Our calling on you must have surprised you," Dev said putting on his shoes.

"Oh, no no," Vijay said. "Anyway, it doesn't matter...."

"It doesn't, and it matters a lot," Dev sighed again.

They walked in silence till they reached the central plinth. Flaming purple clouds had descended into the nearby tank and the inverted Taj lay at their feet, coiling and twisting like a dying serpent. The sunshine clung to the turrets. For a long while Dev kept looking at the expiring image of die Taj. At the other end, Raka was seen coming towards them holding Munmun's hand. But Dev seemed to be oblivious of her. Vijay's eyes roved over him and at Raka and then at the approaching water carrier, from whose bag a stream of water hissed out in a jet like an angry serpent.

"We wanted a witness to soften the agony of our last meeting," Dev said, as if forcing the words. "Yes, a witness, to watch this tension which has reached the snapping point, to share the grim laughter before the spark of joy is extinguished, before the icy shroud of pretensions is torn away. This agony would have been too much for us, alone."

"Mr Dev, what are you driving at?" Vijay was perturbed.

Dev shifted his weight from one foot to the other, looked at Vijay calmly and gave a warm smile. "Mr Vijay, this is our last evening together." He paused, and added: "Raka and I have decided to separate. Our patience has reached its limit. It is better if we part before we lose our heads completely or do something desperate. She's free to marry again if she chooses to.

She can take Munmun with her. I won't stand in her way. If he becomes a burden to her, I am prepared to take him back."

Vijay stood bewildered, blankly gazing at the sleeping image of the Taj in the tank.

"But you must have tried..." Vijay said.

"It's no use."Dev waved his hands impatiently. "We have exhausted all possibilities. We decided to spend the last day together and part as friends." He was silent for a while. "Raka had a great desire to see the Taj," he continued. "We wanted to visit it on our honeymoon. And here we are, on the seventh anniversary of our marriage." He shrugged his shoulders. "Funny, isn't it?"

Vijay felt as if he was standing against the railings of a dam that sent thousands of tons of water thundering down its sluice-gates. He felt dizzy.

"Raka, stop him. The gardener might object. Come here, Munmun." Vijay came to himself. Dev's voice was silken-soft Lifting Munmun in his arms, he snuggled his head in his belly. Munmun was convulsed with pleasure. Raka watched him fondly with love-filled eyes.

Could it be true? Vijay was unable to believe his eyes.

He wanted to see Raka's face. But she had averted her face and was looking into the distance. The evening had advanced and sparrows had started chirping. Stepping closer, Dev whispered in Vijay's ears, "Don't say anything about it to Raka," and then he said apologetically, "Sorry we dragged you here and spoiled your day.

This had happened a couple of years ago, but the event suddenly became vivid in his memory. Dev, Raka, Munmun and he – they were returning in the same manner, quiet, sad and lost. The boat of the evening was about to touch the shore of night, after toiling through a stormy voyage, carrying three tired voyagers who were returning home after a long spell of absence. The elongated shadows of the trees and the buildings had stretched far into the distance. Over the dying sheen of the lawn, white flowers had sparkled into life.

Seeing the Taj Mahals imprinted on Meera's glasses, he had suddenly been reminded of the fateful day, many years ago. It was the same Taj, trembling in the water from behind purple clouds. Had Dev been with him today, how would he have accounted for this situation?

"Did you say something?" Vijay looked at Meera, startled.

"I? No, nothing."

The blanket of silence enveloped them again.

He felt as if they were carrying the mortal remains of a dead moment – its one end in Meera's hand and the other in his – to bury it somewhere in the stillness of the night, afraid lest someone should catch them in the act and brand them assassins. They would fling the dead body behind lonely bushes, and wiping the blood from their hands with scented handkerchiefs, they would get lost in the crowd, afraid of looking at each other.

Outside the precincts of the Taj, they would hire a tonga. The tonga would break into a run, aind as it turned the comer, the Taj would be lost out of sight. "That's the end of it." Like death's rattle, these emaciated words, would escape their dry lips and covering them with the shroud of a pale smile, they would take leave of each other.

7

Under Cover of Darkness

Nirmal Varma

Nirmal Varma, acknowledged as the master of short story in Hindi, was born in Shimla in 1929 and took his Master's degree in History from St. Stephen's College, Delhi. Between 1959 and 1968, he lived in Prague studying and translating Czech literature into Hindi. In Hindi, he has published several novels, collections of short stories and books of essay, travelogues and memoirs. A collection of his stories won him the Sahitya Akademi Award. Another collection of stories, *The World Elsewhere,* was published in England. Considered the pioneer of the short story form in Hindi literature, he breathed his last in October 2005.

Bano had to cut across three goat tracks to reach our house. "Any news?" I was sorely tempted to lie to her and say, "Yes, there is. It's all settled. We'll be leaving for Delhi soon." But I desisted. Bano was too shrewd not to see through my lies. Therefore, I lay silently, with my eyes closed.

As usual, she came over and felt my forehead. When her touch was cold, I knew that my fever had not gone down. But when it was warm, I felt elated. Eagerly opening my eyes I would ask, "Bano, don't you think I am getting better?"

Looking disappointed, she would reply hopefully, "But your temperature is bound to shoot up in the evening!" She was unhappy whenever my temperature came down. She knew that as long as my fever lasted, I could not leave her and would stay put in Simla. Sometimes when I heard her footsteps, I quickly applied a wet towel to my forehead. "Feel my forehead." I would reach out for her hand and brush it against my brow. "Cold, is it?" Without a word, Bano would start looking out of the window.

Outside, one could see the forests, enveloped in a blue haze and lofty mountains, range upon range. When the curtain fluttered in the breeze, the room was full of a dream-like fragrance, wafted frbm afar.

"Beyond those mountains lies Delhi. You know that, of course," I said.

Bano nodded. She had no interest in Delhi, had never been to that city. Her father's office remained in Simla all year round. I pitied her.

"I have been to 'our house'," she said changing the subject.

The mention of 'our house', which on other days had swept me off my feet, today held no interest for me.

"Bano, you can keep my share of plums," I said, without opening my eyes.

"Who would want to eat your rotten plums?" Bano said, peeved. "Take them along when you go to Delhi – your precious cargo of rotten plums!" She went to the verandah.

It made me angry. But when one is ill, one cannot work himself up to a high pitch of anger. In illness, all feelings peter out, without reaching the crescendo of passion. If one cries, no tears come – only the eye-lids flutter. If one feels exhilarated, the heart does not beat faster – only the lips tremble.

The house which Bano had referred to as 'our house' was said to be haunted, and lay deserted all the year. They said an English woman had committed suicide in that house. In one of the bathrooms, we used to store our treasure trove of raw plums and apricots. It was a closely guarded secret and no one was aware of our goings on.

Bano kept swinging in the verandah for a long time. As the swing went up, her *salwar* puffed out like a balloon. The rhythmic creaking of the swing acted like a soporific; I dozed off and had dreams. I always remembered the dreams I had in the afternoons. I dreamed that the *chaprasi* had come from the office to fetch father's lunch. He laughed and told us that we would soon move down to Delhi. Then I saw Bano throwing apricots out of the window of the haunted house. Far away in the hills, I could see the English woman, who had committed suicide, leaning out of the window of the Kalka-Simla train. With outstretched hands, she would grab the apricots which Bano was casting to the winds.

When I woke, Bano had been gone a long time.

In the evening when mother brought in the tea, I asked her if the *chaprasi* had come in the afternoon.

"Yes, he did. Why?"

"Did he tell you anything?"

"No, nothing. What's the matter with you?"

I kept silent. Propping myself up against the pillow, I sipped my tea.

Mother took my temperature and jerked down the column of mercury. I used to insist on being told what my temperature was. But she was reluctant to tell the truth, so I stopped asking. I tried to guess it by watching the expression on her face. Sometimes when I became grave, she would say, "Now get well, and then we shall leave for Delhi." She said it in a casual manner, as if it was entirely up to me to get well or remain ill; as if I was keeping ill out of sheer cussedness and that I had to be cajoled into getting well! This would put me in a temper, and turning on my side, I would lie facing the window. For a long time, she would not realise that I was angry, till I would stiffen my legs, clench my fists, grit my teeth and start breathing heavily. Mother, who had all this while been looking out of the window, would get alarmed. She would look at me intently, sigh and sit down on the bed, by my side. I sensed at once that she had seen through my game, though she never gave me that impression. Taking out a bar of Cadbury's chocolate from the almirah, she would place it under my pillow. "Don't tell your father about it," she would warn me, running her fingers through my hair. But the very next moment, she would forget me; she would be miles away, lost in her own world of thought. I knew this from the way her fingers became inert. The piece of chocolate she had given me was not so much to put me in good humour as to keep me out of her way – so that she could again sink into her shell undisturbed. I would look at her face without her being aware of it. The shadowy lines would be gone, and her face would be a blank emptiness. Her eyes would glow with an inner fire and seem to be misted over with a thin film. I would delude myself into believing that she was thinking of my illness, but in my heart of hearts, I knew that her thoughts had nothing to do with me.

I gently put my hand oh hers. She started as if my touch had dragged her back from some remote recess of her mind. She looked hard at me and then kissed me on the lips. I wiped my mouth with my sleeve. She smiled.

"Child, may I ask you one thing?"

"Yes?"

"If I go away, will you take it amiss?" She looked at me without blinking her eyes.

"Will father go with you?"

"No."

"Then?" I was puzzled.

She started laughing and lay down by my side.

I put my cheek against hers. Mother was very beautiful and everybody was afraid of her. Sometimes I wondered what was that something about her which kept everyone on their toes. I was also afraid of her, though – specially of her eyes when she looked at me closely.

A long time back I once accompanied father to his friend's house. Our path lay along a ravine and as we climbed up we stopped for a while in the forest grove to regain our breath. The silence of the grove felt eerie.

Now when I looked at mother's eyes, I was reminded of that dark forest grove.

Mother's arms were white and smooth as marble. I was shy about touching them. She parted her hair in the middle, sweeping it back tightly, which made her forehead still more prominent. Her ears were small, almost doll-like, and remained hidden under her hair when she lay by my side.

I pulled them out from under her hair and I suddenly remembered that Bano had once told me that people with small ears usually have short lives. I shivered to think of it, but I never told mother. I imagined that when she lay dying I would tell her she was dying before her time because of her ears.

Sometimes I had a feeling that she was not particularly worried over my illness, that perhaps there were times she even forgot I was ill. I also knew that mother was not eager to go to Delhi. Once I heard her saying so to uncle Biren and I wondered why.

For the past few months, mother and father had been sleeping in separate rooms. This seemed odd to me. But then there were many mysteries I did not try to delve into; I simply relegated them to the back of my mind.

Mother's room was at the other end of the gallery and her two windows overlooked mine. Sometimes she could be seen at a window, her hair like molten gold in the sun. I knew she was sitting by the window, reading.

She had many books scattered all over the place – on the sofa, by the pillow, under the bedstead. Perhaps she slept very little. Often I saw the light burning in her room till late in the night.

Once I opened one of her books. On the flyleaf I saw uncle Biren's name inscribed in spidery characters in blue ink. It fascinated me. Later I saw his name on many more books which lay about in her room.

This reminded me of uncle Biren's small cottage which I had visited with mother. One room was chock-a-block with books and there was a step ladder which he used for taking down books from the shelves. The walls of another room were covered with oddly framed paintings before which I would stand and pause for hours. Father told me that uncle Biren had purchased these paintings in Europe before the war. My feelings for uncle Biren were a mixture of wonder and pity. How could he bring himself to live in this lonely cottage all by himself, the year through, winter and summer?

Among father's friends, Uncle Biren had a distinct place of his own. It was only he whom father invited to take tea in my room – others he received in the drawing room. When uncle Biren came, I was not packed off at bed-time. I was allowed to stay on while they sat talking for long hours. They were pleasant evenings.

One evening, when uncle Biren called on us, he was so funnily dressed that for a moment I did not recognise him. Long boots which came up to his knees, a khaki knap-sack slung over one shoulder and a camera over the other, a sola hat, and quaintest of all, a goatee, which did not suit his face. His pockets bulged with books.

He came to my bed and shook hands with me. Uncle Biren was always like that. He always greeted me as one greets a normal, healthy person; and he never wasted his breath in enquiring after my health.

Mother sat beside us, busy knitting. She cast a fleeting glance at Biren and lowered her head. Uncle Biren told us that he was bound for Kufri. He would stay the night in the Rest House and return the following evening. "I am told the watchman of the Rest House has been living in Kufri for the last thirty years." Uncle Biren said, "He must know a lot about Kufri."

A faint smile spread on mother's face. "You have been at this game for more years than one can remember," she said without looking up.

"Oh, so you don't believe me. Then you must look at my notes." Uncle Biren's blue eyes lit up. Somehow any mention of his book, *"A History of Simla"*, always made mother smile.

"Sometimes I come across valuable scraps of information while collecting material for my book," uncle Biren said.

"What kind of information, uncle?" I asked.

I always showed keen interest in uncle's book. It buoyed up his spirits.

"Once I chanced upon an old photograph," uncle Biren said. "An Englishman must have taken it."

"A photograph of...?" mother asked, looking up from her knitting.

"Of a crowd at a race course. Most of the faces were indistinct. But one face, a girl's, had come out clearly. She was standing by the pavilion, an umbrella in her hand. Everyone's eyes were glued to the running horses, but hers seemed to be held by something behind her. A rather incongruous note. Her looking back like that." Uncle Biren suddenly stopped. The knitting lay quite in mother's hands.

"The caption under the photograph read: 'Annadale, Simla – 1903.'

Fifty years ago, And she was still looking back, umbrella in hand."

Uncle Biren laughed, as if at his own whimsey. Mother looked up at him, her eyes icy. Sometimes I wondered why uncle Biren indulged in such meaningless talks.

"At times I feel it is much easier to write about men than about cities," uncle Biren said. "I've assembled a huge mass of notes, old photographs, travelogues on Simla, but I doubt I will ever succeed in writing my book."

"Why?" mother asked.

"Because... because every city is so much absorbed in itself. It does not let you pry into its secrets easily." Uncle Biren got up. He touched my forehead.

"I met the doctor while coming down," he said bending over me. "He said you will be fit enough to walk about in a few days' time."

"Will you just sit up?" he said taking the camera from his shoulder. "I'll take your photograph. Let's see how you look."

After taking my photograph, he picked up his walking stick, ready to leave.

"When will you come again?" mother asked, looking him straight in the eye for the first time.

"Perhaps tomorrow evening... I'll drop in for a minute." When uncle looked at mother, his eyes would look as if dazzled and he would turn his face.

"Uncle Biren..." I said shyly.

"Yes, child?"

"I'll take a photograph."

He smiled and handed me the camera.

I looked at mother.

"No, no, not me, son," she said, her words tumbling over each other.

"You will not be alone. Uncle Biren will also be there." Uncle Biren turned pale and cast a fleeting look at mother. She rose from her chair without any more fuss, saying to me, "You are very wilful."

"Uncle Biren, you stand by the railing – in the sun. And mother, you stand to the right." I climbed out of the bed and stood leaning against the wall. My head reeled. But the photograph was a great success. I have it with me to this day....

I did not know when darkness crept into the room. Uncle Biren had been gone a long time. Only mother was there reclining in a chair by my side – silent and motionless. I did not ask for the light. I like the feeling of darkness slowly invading a room.

Suddenly the memory of a particular evening flitted across my mind. This was much before I fell ill. Mother had taken me to uncle Biren's house.

Uncle Biren was taken aback on seeing us. He let us in through the wicket gate, looking flustered.

"Pono, you here?" It was the first time I heard uncle Biren addressing mother by her name. Coming from his lips, her name rang strangely. Mother started laughing. I don't know why, but I did not like the way she laughed: I felt cramped and a vague numbness spread over my heart.

"We came out for a stroll," mother said, "we thought we might as well say hello to you." It was the first time I heard mother lying.

For a fleeting second uncle Biren's blue eyes clouded with doubt; then he held me by my finger and led us into his cottage.

I saw his library for the first time. He showed me photographs of the mountain peaks of Simla, its valleys and waterfalls. He had collected these for his projected book. A lamp with a light green shade rested on the table by the side of a heap of books. He brought out slabs of chocolate from somewhere. I was not prepared for this sleight of hand, and he laughed at my discomfiture. "I have laid by quite a stock of chocolates," he said. "It comes in handy during winter when I'm snowed in." I looked at uncle Biren. How different from father! He had none of that oppressive grimness and tenseness which I associated with father. There was an intangible tenderness about Uncle Biren. Above his trim beard, the soft eloquence of his eyes seemed to take away the coarseness from everything they ranged over.

"Have you ever seen a snow-capped peak from close range?" he asked me. I shook my head.

"The snow looks blue," he said. "I took a coloured photograph...." He went into the adjoining room. Idly I thumbed through his albums which were lying on a table. Each photograph represented a view of Simla: Glenn, Jakhu, Chetwick Falls. I easily recognised each of these spots! Uncle had not shown up and I began to feel bored. I picked up another album, a small one lying at the corner of a book shelf. I turned the first page, and a known face stared at me. It was a picture of mother.

Was mother ever like this? My heart missed a beat – it was the same broad forehead, but with the small red mark, which mother now does not put on. Two locks of hair fell over her shoulders. She was wearing a full-sleeved sweater, and her small ears were hidden under hair – same as now. Looking at her expression, I had a sudden feeling that that face had nothing to do with me or with father. It was mother, but I could not see my mother in her.

Hearing Uncle Biren's footsteps, I guiltily put away the album.

When we came out on to the lawn, the shadows of the evening had begun to fall. Wrapped in a shawl, mother was sitting on a stone bench. Uncle Biren sat down on the grass near mother's feet. "Where were you all this while?" She tenderly pulled me to her. I looked searchingly into her face. The same eyes, mouth and forehead; separately, they closely resembled her features in the photograph, but together the total impression was different in a way I could not define. Perhaps it was an expression which annihilated distance and yet never came closer.

"What's the matter, son?" Mother ran her fingers through my tangled hair. I shrank into myself and looked away.

Mother did not pay any further attention to me. We sat quietly, lost in our own thoughts. Since our coming, Uncle Biren had not talked with mother. It seemed strange, but its meaning was lost on me.

A blue haze had descended upon the lawn. Among the distant hills, lights shone like glow-worms; the outlines of the hills having been blurred by darkness, the sky seemed to nestle closer to the earth.

While I was ill, I often recalled the evening, although nothing unusual had happened to distinguish it from other evenings. Uncle Biren accompanied us some distance and when mother assured him that we would manage all right, he turned. Swiftly I had gone ahead. I stopped and looked back. Mother was not there. I retraced my steps, peering into the darkness, my heart beating faster.

At the turn of the road. I found mother leaning over the railing, the aid of her sari fluttering in the breeze. She was looking below at Uncle Biren's cottage. In the evening it looked lonely and deserted. A pale streak of light from the library window lay across the lawn.

For a while we stood silent, and then mother resumed her walk. Her gait was so slow that she seemed to be walking in her sleep. When she came up to me, for a long time she stared at me, with helpless eyes. Then she drew me close and put her cold, dry lips to my mouth.

After some days I felt the taste of illness begin to leave my mouth and life seemed to surge back slowly into my limbs. I had the windows opened, and the curtains drawn so that I could bathe in the soft furry warmth of the sunlight.

One morning I came out onto the verandah. A little away from me auntie was busy hanging out her washing on the wooden railing. Stealthily, I crept past her and stepped into the balcony at the back of father's room. The doors and windows of the room at the other end were barred and no curtains were hanging in them. When mother used to go away to her aunt's, father would lock up her room, carry all his things upstairs into the study and spend his nights there.

The balcony looked forlorn. In front of me in the walled compound of the school, I could see small boys, satchels in hand, standing four in a row, reciting their prayers in a nasal sing-song: "God's name comes to my lips with the fervour of a keen desire." Unable to stand their shrill lacerating voices anymore, I looked beyond, over the haunted house across the ravine, and then along the serpentine path which lost itself behind the compound of Bano's house. Fetching father's old discarded walking-stick, at the end of which I had tied a red piece of cloth, I waved above my head. This was a favourite game with me and Bano. She saw me and waved back. Then she pointed me out to her mother, who also waved. Embarrassed, I threw away the stick and ran inside.

Before I could enter my room, a servant came to tell me that father wanted to see me. A wave of joy surged through me. It was rare for father to invite me to his room. Hastily, I bit my nails to make sure that they were clean; father always looked at my nails the first thing.

Father's room had a distinct individuality compounded of the smell of cigar smoke, an oppressive stillness, subdued lighting which did not change with the night or the day; above it all a sour medicinal odour that hung pervasively in the air, like a layer of thinly spread colour.

"What were you doing outside?" I knew father's moods. There was no anger in his voice.

"I was looking for Bano," I fumbled and became silent.

"Father!"

Father looked up.

"I am well now. The fever has left me."

Father placed my hands one upon the other and held them in his big hairy hands. "You must rest in bed a few days more," he said.

"Father, when are we going to Delhi?" It was a question I always asked whenever I met him.

Father removed his cigar from his mouth, and studied the wall-paper, as if he was trying to read something there.

"Son, are you sometimes afraid?"

"Afraid? Afraid of what?" I asked.

Father's eyes turned to me. "I mean, now that your mother is away."

"But she'll be back soon." I hoped father would affirm my statement; but he just looked on expressionlessly and then said 'Yes' in a feeble voice as if speaking to himself.

"Son!"

"Yes, father?"

"Would you like to meet your mother?" His voice sounded hard and his question strange and devoid of meaning. I wanted to say 'Yes' but when I looked at him, I sensed that he wanted me to reply differently, to deliberately lie to him.

I shook my head. He looked at me, surprised, and removed my hands from his lap.

He got up from the chair and went to the window.

As I watched him, I felt sympathy well up in my heart for him. My relations with mother were not hedged with complexity. I did not feel tense and withdrawn with her, as I did with father. She would agree to all my demands without ado. Yet she failed to win my sympathy; whereas, even though I was afraid of father and could not make demands on him or open my heart to him, he touched a chord in my heart. Separating us and mother lay some intangible reality.

Father looked so forlorn. The stillness that reigned in his room seemed to permeate the whole house. Without mother, every room looked empty and desolate.

Mother had left for her aunt's place without seeing me. I happened to wake in the middle of the night before she went.

My room was dark. In the breeze, the window curtain flew up and kept fluttering over my pillow. For some time a doubt hovered in my mind; everything in the room seemed to have shifted from its proper place: the window on my left had quietly moved down to the middle of the wall; the door had slipped two yards to the right. The door was ajar, and from father's room showed a thin mercurial column of light so slender and fragile that a touch would have splintered it to bits. Suddenly, the door flapping like a black birdwing, stood open for a second, then slowly closed. As it closed, a beam of light streaked across the floor and climbed the opposite wall. I heard someone breathing heavily behind the door and I thought it was mother come to fasten the latch. But no one came. I heard voices, now coming from afar; indistinct; wordless sounds. Then so close as if someone were whispering into my ear.

"No, you won't go in." It was father.

A thin cry, like a bright sliver of glass, pierced the heart of darkness: What was wrong with mother? Why did she shriek in this strange manner? "Let go my hand!" she cried.

"Pono, I won't allow you to go in."

"Who are you to stop me? Aren't you ashamed of yourself?"

"Pono, don't shout, he's sleeping."

"I won't shout. Let me go in."

"No, no, not now."

"Do you think I am mad? Do you think I'll tell him ...?"

"Pono, go to your room. You are not in your senses."

Before father could say more, the curtain parted and my bed was flooded with light. I saw two marble like arms spread against the curtain and a shadowy figure with two hungry distraught eyes.... Thin, long fingers clutched the curtain, trembling violently, and a nosepiece shone like a star above quivering lips. I glimpsed the phantasmagoric sight in the fleeting instant before the curtain was pulled across the door. Then there were only muffled groans.

After this, I could not believe my ears. Slow continuous laughter behind the curtain. No, it could not be mother. I had never before heard her laughing like that. I could neither hear nor see anything more. My mind went blank and I felt that the darkness had gathered itself into something tangible, something foul and ragged that coiled and twisted before my eyes.

I was lying on the terrace one afternoon during my convalescence, when no one took any notice of me and I had my way with everything. Father did not drop into my room in the evenings and I had not seen Uncle Biren for a long time. If anyone was sorry about my recovery, it was Bano. Had I remained ill, the chances of our going to Delhi would have receded.

Behind the terrace there were two low hills, pointing towards the sky like a pair of scissors. Between them a forest range stretched far into the distance. When the train bound for Kalka passed through it, a column of smoke drifted above the trees toward the sky.

"Bano, we'll be leaving for Delhi soon," I told Bano who was busy picking apricots from the terrace. Her skirt was filled with apricots. She knelt and her booty spilt on the ground.

"Here, eat this," she said picking up a yellow-ripe apricot. "It's nice."

I shook my head. Father had forbidden me to eat apricots.

"It's ripe, it will do you no harm," she said and without waiting for my answer, popped it into her mouth. She turned the apricot inside her cheek and said that if it was turned often enough, the saliva made the fruit more juicy.

"So it is settled that you are going to Delhi," she said sucking noisily at the apricot

"Yes, as soon as mother returns."

"Where has your mother gone?"

"To her aunt's place."

"Are you sure?" Bano looked at me mysteriously.

"What's the matter, Bano?" I asked, puzzled.

"Nothing. Just asking." She pressed the apricot between her lips and added, "Won't tell you. Mother has warned me not to."

I felt angry but smiled, feigning indifference. When I was angry, I tried to hide my feelings behind a smile so that no one would think I was an ill-tempered fool.

The hills behind the terrace were grey under the lowering clouds and their thin elongated shadows flitted across them from the cast.

"Is Delhi beyond those mountains?" Bano asked me.

"Delhi is in the plains." I replied. "One has to climb over those hills to reach Delhi."

Bano looked at me sceptically. "But below us is the Annandale Race Course, and beyond that the ravine. Is Delhi in the ravine?"

Without trying to satisfy her curiosity, I turned my back on her.

Near the terrace was the pavilion and behind the pavilion the guest room of the haunted house. Bano threw the apricot stones into the guest room and stood leaning against the wall.

All Simla lay hushed in the afternoon; only the sound of falling apricots punctuated the silence. Bano beckoned me to her. The glass of one of the guest house doors was broken. She peeped through the hole and invited me to join her.

The room was empty, its wall-paper faded. It was full of stale air and cobwebs. In the middle of the floor there was a small circle of light which seemed to change from white to faded yellow and back again. In the darkness, the spot of light looked eerie.

"That English woman must have lived in this room," Bano whispered.

"And she must have died in this room," I added and a shiver ran down my spine. I saw a face gradually emerging on the peeled off plaster of the wall – its mouth gaped and its lustreless eyes seemed to mock me, and I heard laughter. It must have been the face of the woman who had taken her own life here, years ago... her laughter reminded me of mother's laughter that night.

"Bano, did your mother tell you something about my mother?"

"How does that concern you?"

The doors of the deserted house rattled in the wind.

"Bano, when I was ill, sometimes I had strange feelings. I felt I was also like mother – that there was something common between us. Something which no one likes to talk about. I saw an apparition wrapped in snow, whose hands were white as marble and always remained dangling in the air. An apparition which coming from behind suddenly bottled me up – and then I fell apart from my own self. Yes, from my own being, Bano!"

Bano shook like a leaf and her eyes grew wide with fear.

We were all packed and ready to leave. Labels had been pasted on all the boxes, bags and bed-roll – "Simla-Delhi," and father's name in bold letters below. The servants and peons from father's office ran all over the place, busy with the arrangements; the house bustled with activity.

Mother was in her room upstairs, doing nothing. Father had asked me not to go to her; perhaps she was not well. I had not met her since she returned from her aunt's place. She had arrived at night when I was asleep.

Having nothing to do, I knocked about the house till I felt suffocated with boredom. Keeping out of the way, I escaped from the house.

Descending the footpath, I started along the ravine, picking pine cones till both my pockets were stuffed with them. On the distant hills the late sunlight still lingered, too tired to merge into darkness.

I had come a long way from home and, when I started walking back, I suddenly spotted Uncle Biren's tiny cottage, down below, cosily ensconced in a cluster of trees. I remembered that particular evening when I had come to the cottage with mother. Since the time mother had gone to stay with her aunt, Uncle Biren had stopped calling on us. Once I had asked father about Uncle Biren. But his expression had become so hard that I dared not pursue the subject.

I walked down to the cottage. In the westering sun, the sloping roof had become a glowing red. The wicket gate was open. I tiptoed on to the lawn. The wind sighing through the grass deepened the sense of desolation. At the edge of the lawn I could see the stone bench on which mother had sat.

I gently knocked at the door, "Uncle Biren, Uncle." My voice went ringing through that lonely, mute cottage. I felt it was not my own voice, but an unfamiliar one, which chased my own.

"Come in. The door is unlocked."

I went in. The dim light of the table lamp fell on the books and the papers which lay in disorder on the table. Uncle Biren asked me to sit on his bed and pulled up his easy chair beside me.

"Have you walked alone, this long distance?" He took my hand in his and smiled.

Suddenly his eyes fell upon my bulging pocket and I went red in the face.

"What have you in those pockets of yours?" he asked me. "Pine cones?"

I nodded.

"What will you do with them?"

"They are for the train."

"For the train?" Biren Uncle's face had become a question mark.

"Yes, we are leaving for Delhi tonight, uncle."

He looked at me without blinking. Then he got up and without taking further notice of me, started gazing out of the window. A suffocating silence filled the room. I felt he had already known about our going away. When he turned from the window, his blue eyes shone.

"You remember the photograph you took that day?" he asked me. "It's ready. Would you like to see it?"

He took out an envelope from the almirah and handed it to me. "You are quite an expert," he said "the photograph has come out very well."

I looked at the photograph. The event, which I had consigned to the limbo, returned vividly.

Against a hazy backdrop of mountains, I saw Uncle Biren standing close to the railing of the balcony, his arm unknowingly touching mother's sari. And mother... she stood with half-closed eyes, her lips parted, as though she was on the point of uttering something, and had then abruptly checked herself.

I kept looking at the photograph for a while.

Then I was reminded of the train journey which I had to make. I climbed off the bed. "Well, Uncle..." I was too overwhelmed to unburden my thoughts.

Uncle Biren came close to me. He touched my hair and gently kissed me on the forehead – the same way mother had kissed me that night.

We came out.

"May I see you home?" he asked me.

I shook my head. I knew the way. For a while we stood silent in the verandah.

"Son...." Startled, I looked at him.

"Your mother once wanted a book. I forgot about it...." He hesitated.

"Please give it to me. I'll take it with me."

While handing me the book, I thought he wanted to say something, but could not.

The cottage was left behind. I made my way back, along the deserted road. When I neared home, I stopped under a lamp-post and examined the book.

The envelope containing the photograph was lying within its pages.

The book was very old. Even today I can vividly recall its yellow and brittle pages – *Flaubert's Letters to George Sand*. Those days I was not familiar with the names of Flaubert or

George Sand. Years after, when I read the book, mother was no more, and Uncle Biren had long since left the country and settled in Italy.

But that day the book had no significance for me. For a long time I stood under the lamp-post, holding the book and looking. to the room upstairs.

The window of mother's room was closed, but a sepulchral light shone through.

That was our last evening in Simla.

8

The Mark of Man

Himanshu Joshi

Himanshu Joshi was born in 1935 in the Kumaon hills, and forged ahead as a writer of great promise. His first collection of stories was published in 1965 and he has seven novels and eighteen collections of stories to his name. His widely acclaimed stories have been published under the title *Ikyawan Kahanian.* He writes with equal felicity on city and rural life. One of his novels has been made into a film. He has been widely translated into various Indian and European languages. He breathed his last in November 2018.

The water had caught fire. There was an uproar in the village. The people were reluctant to believe it; yet the news passed from mouth to mouth. Kirpua had done it with Govindi. It was a matter of great shame. Kishnava's wife had seen it with her own eyes.

Her body covered with a tattered sheet, Govindi was sitting huddled up, shedding tears. Her aged blind father was sitting in a dark comer of his thatched shed, blowing smoke from a chillum which was on the point of going out.

"Oh Perma!" people spat out the words at him as they passed by his shed. "What a daughter! You should have drowned yourself before you begot her. You've brought a bad name to the entire community. You'll do well to push her into a pit and burn her alive. An immoral girl like her has no right to live."

Perma's grip on the coconut chillum tightened, showing the stringlike nerves oil his gnarled hand. He took a few quick angry puffs at the chillum, filling the shed with smoke. He feared he would go crazy before the evening approached. He might even die. Even if he did not die, people would not spare him. They would twist his neck and squeeze the life out of him. Not that he was afraid of dying. But to be killed! The thought was so horrifying that he shrank into himself.

A few people standing outside the shed idly watched the scene. Leaving their chores, some women of the neighbourhood came out to have a good look at Govindi. Some elders of the village settled themselves on the flat stones forming the plinth of the courtyard. They were sagely applying their minds to the "delicate" problem in hand.

"If Govindi had resisted Kirpua, he wouldn't have dared touch her body, much less take liberties with her. She must have made a tell-tale gesture the fellow could not resist. Which young man could resist temptation? A woman is a woman, you know!" said one elder.

"Poor girl, she's not to blame," said another elder. "It runs in the family of the one-eyed Gangua. This fellow steals grain from his house and sells it off. And then he goes about with loafers."

"This degenerate will have it fair and square in the next world," an old man cursed Kirpua. "What does he mean by casting an evil eye on another's daughter? The goddess Tenura will make him burn in hell fire." Govindi was in her twenty-first year. Ten years ago, when she was eleven, her husband had passed away. He had gone into the forest to graze his sheep and fell foul of a wolf in broad daylight

After her marriage, Govindi had not even been to her in-law's house once. She didn't know what a husband meant to a woman; it was only a concept to her. Govindi had no brother or sister and had spent all these years in her father's house like a lone bird. Every day she paved the vestibule with mud, sprinkled water on the tulsi plant and fed the morsel of roti to the cow. Not even by mistake did she exchange a glance with anyone. Nor did she look anyone in the face. And today, all eyes were turned on her. She was too confused to know what to make of the situation. If someone asked her how it happened, she would just start crying.

"Yes, how did it happen?" they would ask. Even those who knew, wanted to know again; it gave them vicarious pleasure to see her sitting there like a mute-dumb or sinking into the earth out of shame.

The morning was hectic. It was late in the afternoon when the *sarpanch* appeared on the scene. People gathered round him like bees swarming round the beehive. There was a cold breeze blowing, it was likely to snow at night. But people did not mind staying out under the inclement sky.

At last the quorum was complete and the *panchayat* went into session.

"Has anyone witnessed the man doing the 'bad act' with Govindi?" the sarpanch asked.

"Yes, Kishnava's Ija saw it," someone from among the crowd replied.

"Where did she see it?"

"In the cattle shed."

"Why did Kishnava's Ija go there?"

"She had gone there to milk her cow."

"When did she go there? Morning or evening?"

"In the evening."

The people in the crowd looked at one another's face.

"Where's Kishnava's Ija? Call her here." The sarpanch who was sitting cross-legged to assert his importance, visibly expanded in his seat like a rich moneylender. An appropriate frown formed between his eyebrows.

"She has gone to her younger daughter's house at Kalhot. She left this morning."

"What did she say she saw there?"

"That the black-faced Kirpua was doing the shameful act with Govindi."

"Didn't Govindi resist?" There was no reply from the audience.

"In what state was Govindi at that time?" The sarpanch directed the question to the man squatting in front of him, who claimed to know about the whole affair.

The man, confused, looked at the sarpanch and scratched his bald head.

"Her condition must be bad," he ventured a reply at last.

"How bad?" No one came forward with an answer.

"In what condition was Kirpua?" the sarpanch persisted with his questioning.

"He should also be in a bad condition," a comparatively young member of the panchayat suddenly blurted out. A hush fell over the audience.

"When Kishnava's Ija saw what was going on there, why didn't she raise an alarm?"

"It was for Govindi to raise an alarm," said one of the members of the panchayat.

"No!" the sarpanch banged his fist on the paved platform. "The panchayat is of the opinion that both should have raised an alarm. Both are guilty in the eyes of the panchayat."

Soon Govindi was brought before the panchayat. She was wearing tattered clothes and all eyes were fixed on those parts of her body which showed through the holes in her clothes – like patches of sunshine. Govindi shrank into herself.

"What did Kirpua do with you?"

No answer.

"When he caught your body, why didn't you raise an alarm?"

No answer.

"Was Kirpua alone at that time? Or there were others with him?" Silence.

"Kishnava's Ija says that she had seen both of you coming out of the shed. You were creeping away, taking shelter beneath the trees. Kirpua had jumped down from the mound into the field below."

Govindi stood silently before the panchayat. The sarpanch was annoyed. He rebuked and then threatened her, trying to strike fear into her heart. But Govindi stood there with her head lowered like a dumb-mute.

Turning to the people standing around him, the sarpanch continued with his catechism.

"Has anyone of you seen Govindi going about with Kirpua?" he asked.

"Yes." A voice from the audience. It was Khilva's elder brother, Rudia.

"Where did you see them together?"

"In the field," Rudia replied.

"What were they doing there?"

"Govindi was standing near her orange tree while I was grazing my calf.

"I saw Kirpua coming along, driving his bullocks. He looked at Govindi and smiled. 'Govindi, give me some oranges, I'm thirsty,' he said. Govindi plucked an orange and gave it to him. 'They are sour,' Kirpua curled up his nose. 'Give me some ripe ones, the juicy ones.' 'They are not ripe *yet*. They are all sour,' Govindi replied. 'You have ripe ones. But you're hiding them.' He laughed and Govindi also sniggered."

The sarpanch looked at Govindi and then at the papers lying in front of him. "Call Kirpua," he ordered.

He was told that Kirpua had sold his horse and had gone away to Mandi Bhabbar early in the morning. He had taken his saw with him.

The sarpanch looked at the aiudience dumbfounded – as if his prize quarry had escaped his clutches.

The night was advancing. People stood shivering in the cold. Many had returned home and the others were looking for an opportunity to slip away.

"It seems she is feeling shy," the sarpanch looked at Govindi. "She won't make a statement in the presence of others." His eyes flitted over the faces of the other members of the panchayat, as if he were trying to read their minds. "I must ask her a few questions in private. Otherwise, this enquiry will remain inconclusive."

All of them nodded their heads in approval and Govindi, who had gone a few steps, suddenly stopped in her tracks.

The sarpanch took her aside and asked her a few questions. After he had finished, the other members of the panchayat interrogated her.

In the morning, the sarpanch was ready with his judgement. The panchayat in whom god resides was unanimously of the view that Kirpua had done 'wrong' by Govindi. He deserved to be transported for life, if not sent to the gallows. Hence, it was a case fit to be handed over to the police.

Three days later, the *Patwari* descended upon the village with his retinue. As he stepped into the village, he roared like a lion and menacingly waved his hand in the air. It was a heinous crime. Under what section of the Indian Penal Code had this blasted panchayat sat in judgement over these blokes without seeking his permission? They had no business to poke their noses into this affair. None below the rank of a Patwari was authorised to deal with a case such as this.

The people of the village were stunned. They were not as scared of a man-eater as they were of a Patwari who was regarded as an important limb of the law.

In the evening, the Patwari gave Perma a sound thrashing for not keeping his young daughter under his thumb. Why did he allow her to go out of the house, he wanted to know. Since Kirpua was missing from the village, having thought it expedient to go away to Bhabbar then, the Patwari called his mother and made it very clear to her that unless she produced her son before him, forthwith, she would be handcuffed. He suspected that she had a hand in this affair. As testified by the village people, she had instigated her son to abscond from the village. She would now have to appear before the court – an unthinkable thing for a woman who considered herself respectable. But this could not be helped, for law was law.

Trembling with fear, Kirpua's mother begged the Patwari for mercy and kept standing before him with folded hands.

The Patwari banged his shoe, which was split at the toe, on the bare back of the sarpanch, making it clear to him that he could be dethroned from his official pedestal because of his stupid and thoughtless handling of Govindi's case. The sarpanch stood before him in abject surrender. Having dealt with these people, the Patwari sent for Govindi.

"They say you've spoilt the whole village," he thundered at her. "That *haramzada* Kirpua is not a bad sort, but you lured him into doing bad things. Tell me, haven't you? If you are bursting with youthfulness, why don't you go in for a regular husband?"

Govindi fell at the Patwari's feet and said that she was not at fault. She had done nothing 'bad'. They had refused to give her asylum in her late husband's house and she had to return to her father's house where she lived in utter servility.

"When were you forced into doing that?"

She kept looking at the Patwari speechless.

"How many more people were with him?"

She was silent.

"What was your father doing at that time?"

Silence.

"Where did the fellow lead you, holding your hand?"

No reply.

"How long was he with you?"

Govindi sat inert like an earthen pitcher, only tears rolled down her eyes.

The Patwari was in a fix. He didn't know how to handle this case. The more he questioned Govindi, the more she cried. He wiped the beads of cold sweat from his forehead, and, like a shrewd man came to the conclusion that the manner in which he was conducting the investigation would only lead him to a dead end. It was a complicated case. Before preparing his report, it was incumbent upon him to inspect the site of the occurrence and make a sketch of it. To prepare his report without any interference, the Patwari decided to retire to the cowshed with Govindi so that he would interrogate her further.

Govindi followed him gingerly. The people watched the Patwari with fearful eyes from behind their doors as he passed by their houses. They feared that if the culprit was not hauled up in time the following day, the entire village would be rounded up for a wholesale beating.

"Where were you when that rascal came here?" The Patwari's voice boomed through the cowshed in the dark. Govindi cowered before him and then fell back. There was no other person around. The Patwari led Govindi towards the other comer near the heap of hay.

"Show me the spot where you were standing at that time."

Govindi looked at him with a blank face.

"Describe the manner in which he caught you." The Patwari lowered the wick of his lantern and put it aside.

"He must have jumped down like this." The Patwari jumped down from the heap of hay like a cat.

"Then he must have caught you like this from behind." To demonstrate the culprit's action, he caught Govindi from behind.

"Then he must have pulled you down over the hay and made you lie down on it." The Patwari pulled her down with a jerk over the hay.

"You must have watched him helplessly, too scared even to scream." Govindi watched the Patwari in utter bewilderment, without putting up any resistance, her jaws taut, her lips clenched.

After some time, the Patwari got up brushing the hay from his clothes. "Let's go," he said' in a brusque voice. "My inspection is over.

"Tomorrow I'll ask one of the men to come over and prepare the sketch. Kirpua has certainly erred. He must be sent to the gallows for it."

The Patwari's real job was over. But he was still not satisfied. So early next morning, he asked the villagers to assemble and then beat them up.

He called them into his room, one by one, and his *lathi* would menacingly hover before their eyes before it seared their flesh.

In this 'community beating', when the Patwari's lathi fell with a whack upon Andev's bald pate, he trembled from head to foot and urinated in his discoloured patched-up pajamas – the urine running down his legs in a rill.

"I want to dig deep into this nasty incident," the Patwari thundered. "Out with the truth! Otherwise, I'll stuff your body with hay."

The Patwari slapped him hard, five finger marks were imprinted on Andev's cheek.

Of their own accord, Andev's trembling hands joined up together. "Sarkar ! You're my mai bap!"

"You bloody son of sarkar! I want to know the truth. Who did it? Kirpua of someone else?"

"No, it wasn't Kirpua, sarkar!"

"Then who did it?"

"Narda Padhan did it."

"But with whom? Who was the woman?" The Patwari's eyes became big with surprise.

"With Kishnava's Ija."

"Then why was Govindi's name dragged in?"

"People say," Andev's voice shook "...that Govindi had seen them doing it together in his barn. Fearing that she may spill the beans, they tried to implicate her. They were all party to it."

For some time the Patwari watched Andev in silence as if stunned at the new turn of events. Then the lathi fell whack upon Andev's thighs. "You dog! You ass," the Patwari cried. "I know your brain is addled. You son of an idiot, tell me how Kirpua comes into the picture!"

At a loss for an answer, Andev kept sitting stiffly on his haunches, blankly eyeing the Patwari. Then he had a brain-wave. "Sarkar, he went to Bhabbar in the morning. So they thought they would mention his name."

"Where's that bitch now? That hussy! Kishnava's Ija?" The Patwari gnashed his teeth.

"Sarkar, she has gone to her younger daughter's home. She will spend the winter there."

The Patwari kicked Andev hard and pushed him violently. He tumbled down the stairs. After some time Narda Padhan was brought in, his hands tied behind his back with a string. The Patwari flipped a stem of poison ivy against his naked back. He groaned and squirmed with pain as the stem seared his flesh.

"Sala, how he groans!" The Patwari dragged Narda near him. "Tell me? What did you do with Kishnava's Ija?"

"Sarkar, I did nothing with her," Narda whined. "She's like a sister to me." He started crying. "I can't even think of doing such a thing with her."

"Then with whom did you do it?" The Patwari looked angrily at Narda.

"With Khilva's Bojeu." Narda said after a grim silence, giving himself time to weigh the matter.

The Patwari sent for Khilva's Bojeu. After a good deal of prodding, Bojeu said that it was not Narda but her husband's younger brother. A messenger was rushed to fetch Khilva's younger brother. He said that he was just having some innocent fun with Bojeu. But it was Rukhali with whom he was actually having an affair.

"Where's Rukhali now?"

"At her husband's house."

"Besides yourself, with whom else is she having an affair?"

"With Tikua."

"Where's Tikua?"

"He's in his field harvesting the crop."

"Ask that swine to report here, fast!"

Tikua dismissed Rukhali with a shrug. Instead, he mentioned the name of another woman who was dead.

In the course of three days, after beating twenty-seven persons, the Patwari succeeded in unmasking thirty clandestine affairs. When he disclosed his intention of sending the errant fools to the police lock-up, the whole village trembled with fear. Washing the Patwari's feet with their tears, the culprits placed twenty rupees each at his feet. Duly appeased, the demi-god departed from the village.

The night had still to run its course when they saw the *Peshkar's* peon, Dev Singh, standing under a pine tree flourishing a yellow piece of paper.

The village people realised that the government had got to the bottom of the truth. The lid was off the wily machinations of the sarpanch and the Patwari. The Peshkar had done it. There was a running feud between the Peshkar and the Patwari. The former had pulled appropriate strings in high quarters and had had the case re-opened. Through him the Tehsildar and the Collector had got the hang of the real thing.

To straighten out the matters the old Peshkar, Bechi Singh, who looked most imposing in his gray pointed moustache, had arrived in the village, his cronies in tow.

The people were called again to line up, and, the investigations began anew. The wicked Patwari had played dirty with the poor villagers. The Peshkar, the wad went round, would leave no stone unturned to expose the Patwari and to have him removed from his job. He was doing this in the interest of the villagers so that they could live in peace.

Calling the villagers, one by one, he spoke to them softly and then spat into their faces. As a result, one refrain ran through their individual statements. The Patwari, they slated, had intimidated them out of their wits and made them shell out money – although they could hardly afford to do so. Not stopping at that, he had a goat butchered for his meal and had forced women of the village to lie with him. Of course, they had seen it with their own eyes. And, worst of all, he had emptied one big container of liquor, all of which found its way down his gullet.

"How many goats did that son of a bitch devour?" the Peshkar asked, his eyes blazing like live charcoal.

"Hazoor, one big ram and one lamb."

"Whose ram was it?"

"Hazoor, Padia's."

"Ask that bloody fool to show up at once!"

"And whose lamb was it?"

"Chunia's. The one who has his house at the end of the village."

"Call that damn fool also!"

Both the 'fools' were soon ushered into the august presence of the Peshkar. They stood before him in grim silence, their bones rattling with fear.

"Did you *badmashes* offer your goats to the Patwari?"

They tried to answer, but the sound died in their throats. The Peshkar repeated his question, but they were too overawed to speak. Terribly worked up, the Peshkar started beating them until his arms ached and they lay before him, grovelling in the dust. He had them clapped in the barn nearby and had its door latched from outside.

"Who among you had the audacity to bribe the Patwari?" His eyes went from one person to the next.

"Ganganand," one of them whispered in a faint voice.

It transpired that Ganganand had gone to a neighbouring village where he had been invited by a client to eat at his house.

The Peshkar was unrelenting. Word was sent to Ganganand, asking him to return to the village.

"Ganganand, did you bribe that scoundrel? Swine! Don't you know it's as much a crime to give a bribe as to accept it?"

Before Ganganand could reply, a resounding slap fell on his withered cheek. Then another and a third.

Panting hard, Ganganand started frothing at his mouth.

"I'm not alone in it." At last he managed to spew out the words. "The others also bribed the Patwari."

Holding Ganganand's ear like a puppy's, the Peshkar made him rise from the ground and had him locked up in the barn. Others also met a similar fate. Having disposed of them, the Peshkar proceeded to inspect the barn where Kirpua was reported to have done the 'bad' act with Govindi. Govindi was a widow – a most helpless creature. The Peshkar's heart oozed with pity for her.

He was prepared to go one step further. He would not only have the Patwari removed from his job, he would also have him hanged publicly.

He called Govindi into his room and making her sit by his side asked her, in words cloying with sympathy: "Tell me, what did the Patwari do with you?"

Govindi sat wordless. Drawing closer to her, the Peshkar fondled her hair. "Why don't you speak?... What did that mean fellow do with you? When? How? And how many times?"

Unable to bear the weight of his sympathy, Govindi sat silent, holding her head between her thighs like a child.

The Peshkar's heart melted. He pulled her to himself, his fingers feeling the soft flesh of her body.

"The sarpanch was cruel to you. And so was the Patwari. The sarkar has come to know about everything. They will be put in jail for life. The sarkar is annoyed with them. I'm angry with them. Everybody is angry with them. I'll have the Patwari's skin flayed by a cobbler and stuff his body with hay. I'll have you rewarded by the sarkar. You're a good girl. Docile like a cow. Very docile."

The Peshkar's breathing became strained. He flung his arms around her and then fell upon her.

9

The Encircling Clouds

Krishna Sobti

Krishna Sobti was born in Punjab in 1925 and was educated at Shimla, Lahore and Delhi. Her forte was the short story, though she also distinguished herself in her novels which were marked by a virile diction and a bold approach, characteristically her own. She was very versatile in her writing and has acquired a high standard or virtuosity. She won both the Sahitya Akademi Award and the Sahitya Shiromani Award in 1980.

Lying in a small cottage at Bhowali Sanatorium, I look at the hills stretching away in front of me. I look at the encircling clouds, swollen with rain, and at the barren ones, wisp-like and shrivelled. I look at the mist groping in vain, and at my own body, bare to the bones like a tree shorn of leaves in autumn. In front, the path to Ramgarh is etched into the rank vegetation of the sloping mountain, like a thick vein on my arm. The breeze, wayward like my own breath, now caresses and now pummels at the window. My body tucked inside the blanket gradually disintegrates like a thin layer of lime slowly dissolving in water, and I live in constant dread of my life woven with the warp and woof of long years, suddenly missing its pulse beat.

Time drags on – morning, evening and then an unending night descends on me with a long yawn. And I always find myself in this bed – as if since eternity. The curtains at the door and the windows always hang listlessly, silent like me. Nobody lifts them with firm hands and stands at the threshold to greet me with a smile. Oblivious of nights and days, I lie in the iron-bed and look at myself, at my wasting body from which life is ebbing away and moan at my helplessness, the only asset which I now possess. Nothing else remains.

My life was not an arid waste like this. It glowed with joy and knew loving companionship. I look at my thin arms sticking out of my shoulders and am reminded of those plump arms, that perfumed hair, and those soft lips which gave me life. Early in the morning someone would bend over my bed and say, "Won't you get up? It's morning."

With sleep-heavy eyes, I would encircle my arms round her and mumble, "Where's the hurry?"

Breakfast in the garden. The mistress of the house, chic and debonair, confident of her authority, would create the illusion of turning the dreams of the night into tangible reality. I would look at her fingers while she poured milk into the cup, those fingers which had caressed my hair in the night, and the end of her sari jealously hiding her gently heaving breasts. For a fleeting moment I would wonder if what I felt deep down in my being was merely the outer trappings and that the reality lay somewhere still deeper, in those transient moments where two beings became me.... And then came another night at the sanatorium, bleak and dark. Lying under the blanket, I look at the vials of medicine, read their labels over and over again, and realize that when the sap of life dries up, bones and flesh become wood – not earth, because from the earth life sprouts once again.

In the vacuity of this dreary existence I try to resurrect that memorable night when on receiving a message I hurried to her room. Under the blue light of the lamp, two tired eyelids fluttered, and after gazing at an infant, sleeping in the crook of an arm, two eyes came to rest on my face. I got up and touched her cold brow with my lips, and marvelled at how love that permeates the mind can also take a human form, the flesh of my flesh.

But there is another form of love which never came to fruition, like the mountain clouds which promise rain but never break into a shower.

It was years ago. I had gone to the hills during summer. One bright morning we had just got up from the breakfast table when my aunt introduced me to her. I still remember those beautiful eyes. "Ravi, meet Manno. She's here just for two days." My aunt's introduction lacked warmth. A sigh escaped her lips. There was something bitter about the way my aunt said that she was here for two days. I didn't like it.

She acknowledged my greeting with a slight bow and I perceived a faint smile on her face. Thin but lively, her face wore a far-off expression. I could not take my eyes off her face. Her hair tightly swept back seemed to atone for someone's transgression.

When we came out, aunt's children became playful. They tugged at Manno's sari and clung to her arms and cried, "Mannoji, Mannoji..." My aunt about to go in, turned round on hearing the shrill laughter of the children. I still remember her face as she tried to hide her stem expression. With a firm hand she pulled away the children. Looking coldly at Manno, she said in a limp voice, "Manno, better go out for a stroll. These children will not let you alone." Seeing the reproach in their mother's eyes, the children ran off.

My aunt's arms fell by her sides. Manno looked at her steadily.

But before my aunt could get over ter discomfiture, Manno was out of the gate.

'Tell me, bua," I asked my aunt, "What's this mystery?"

My question had apparently irritated her. "She's ill, Ravi," she said shortly, and then added, "For the last two years, she has been staying at the sanatorium. Now her father has bought her a cottage there; an old family servant looks after her. When she gets fed up with the place, she comes to the city for a brief spell."

I was too shocked to believe her words.

"Ravi, when I see her on her rare visit, I lose my appetite."

"But you shouldn't have sent the children away so abruptly," I said trying to probe her further. "Didn't you see she felt hurt?"

My aunt looked hard at me, as if she thought it futile to explain things to me, and went inside. The children were busy playing. I stood there puffing at a cigarette, trying to blow away my vague apprehensions with the curling smoke. How suffocating and bleak her life must be! I walked out of the gate and climbing down the ridge took the road running along the bank of the lake. In the sunlight, little waves shimmered and broke against the bank. I stopped in front of the Naini Temple, and leaned against the railing to watch the boats. In one boat two young men, rowing with rawboned hands, sped past towards Tallital, leaving behind an old man dozing in another boat. Then followed a few European women in the club's boat.

Turning away from the railing I looked in the direction of my aunt's house. The Cheena Peak stood firm in its exalted glory, looking down at me.... I stood on the road bewildered. Everything was the same as on other days, but for two eyes, their image imprinted deep in the caverns of my mind, and that illness behind those eyes, inaccessible and beyond release.

My aunt had gone out with the children. I went into the drawing room, and having nothing better to do, looked at the decor and admired my aunt's taste. On the cabinet stood the family photograph, in a heavy frame. What was there so attractive about my aunt's husband that she doted on him so much? But no, it was unbecoming of me to harbour such thoughts in my aunt's own house....

I climbed the stairs to my room. Lighting a cigarette, I gazed out of the window. Bright-red tin roofs dotted the hills and grey hill tracks meandered over them. Aunt would be back soon.... And Manno. I kept turning the pages of an old magazine.

"May I lay the table Saheb?"

"When will aunt be back?"

"She said she won't take her lunch."

"And the guest?"

"She will lunch alone. Upstairs."

I crushed the cigarette under my foot, relieved that I would not be tortured by her presence – or was it at my helplessness that I could not keep company with her? What else passed through my mind I do not remember. All that I remember is that I toyed with my food absent-mindedly and kept looking out.

I was at the end of my last course when I heard hoof-beats.

"Will you be able to reach me there in two hours?" The voice was low but firm.

"Yes, Hazoor."

I heard her going upstairs. Lunch was over, but I did not get up. Even after helping myself to another cup of coffee, I kept sitting at the table. It struck me that to be disturbed by such a brief encounter was a sign of terrible weakness. Why should a casual introduction make me so restless?

But after an hour, I found myself climbing the stairs. A curtain hung across the open door. I knocked.

"Please come in," Manno was standing by her suitcase, holding a Cashmere shawl. She did not lose her composure on seeing me. "Please sit down," she said, removing things from the sofa.

This was the brightest room in aunt's house. New furniture, costly curtains and Manno wearing a light yellow sari. It cheered me.

"You've had your lunch, of course?" I asked just for the sake of saying something.

"Yes."

"Is aunt out?"

Manno nodded. She folded the shawl and put it in the suitcase, saying, "I'll be gone before the evening. Please tell aunt I came for a day only."

"But she'll be back soon."

She said nothing, nor indicated anything by her expression.

"Won't you stay for another day?" I asked.

Silently, she bent over her suitcase, putting things into it. After a pause she said, laughing, "What's the use? This small city holds no attraction for me after a big village like Bhowali." After so many years, her laughter still rings in my ears and the pallor of her face is still vivid in my mind.

We came down together, I carrying her coat on my arm. The servant and the gardener bowed and were given tips. The syce patted the horse.

"Will you ride?"

With a fleeting glance she looked at the coat. "No, I would rather walk. Lead the horse."

I wanted her to ride, but could not force the words out of my mouth. At the gate she turned her head as if she was taking a last look at the house. She quickly collected herself and started off briskly down the slope. We walked in silence.

Her things were put in the taxi. The driver sensed the tense situation. "Shall we start?" he asked.

With a blank look she stretched her hand for the coat. As she sat down in the car, the attendant took a rug and with professional dexterity spread it over her knees. "Anything else, Memsaheb?"

The curly head fell listlessly back. "That's all, thanks." She laid her thin arms feebly on her knees.

She looked tired. I could see the fish-faced golden bangles on her wrists. But what was in her eyes? – I could not make out for the life of me. She was looking steadily at her hands lying inert on her knees.

The car started and I looked back. No arms were raised, no lips moved in farewell. Till the car disappeared around the bend, I kept looking at the ribbon innocently tied round her hair falling at the nape, visible from the window screen.

Even today when I conjure up those moments, my heart turns numb. After the road had swallowed up the speeding car, I turned back and trudged along the bank of the lake. In vain I tried to blot out her face, but it kept bobbing up before my eyes, again and again. It was a slow ascent to the house, halting and weary. The thought of it tires me even today. The coolies were shifting the furniture on the verandah. Something clutched at my heart. So it was all a game, a make-believe! Manno's room had been furnished with hired furniture. I saw aunt in a new light; the impression that I had formed about her was suddenly wiped out. My aunt was standing at the door. "Ravi go and wash," she said in a constrained voice. "Tea will be ready in a minute. Don't be late."

We sat down to tea. The children were not about. Only my aunt. She poured tea and pushed the cup towards me.

"Aunty?"

She pretended she had not heard me.

"Aunty," I said again, "Why did our visitor leave so abruptly? She had come for two days, right?"

Aunt kept stirring her tea. Her silence drove me wild.

"She asked me to tell you that a day's stay was enough for her."

Why do I think of all this now? Why these futile thoughts?

Gripped by a vague nervousness, I hurried down. I switched off the light and tumbled into my bed. Lying awake I thought of that small cottage in Bhowali where Manno would have reached by now.

"Ravi!"

It was my aunt. She came and sat down by my side and fondled my hair. Then for a moment her hand became still and then passed over my brow. "I'm not fondling you but that unfortunate girl," she said in a trembling voice. "This hand will never touch her again."

My hand trembled in her grasp. I felt I was holding Manno's hand.

"Ravi, stop thinking of her. She'll not be in our midst for long."

I trembled at my aunt's touch. "Aunty, I may not live long either." Today years later, lying in a cottage in Bhowali, I think countless times what made me utter those prophetic words, whose horrid truth I feel in my pulse-beats, day after day and night after night. I don't know how aunt reacted to those words. But I remember her suddenly switching on the lights and looking full in my face with reproachful eyes. "Have you gone crazy?" she said. "Do you want to align your fate with a girl who gropes in a blind alley and for whom there is no point of return?"

She sat down in the chair. "Ravi, you have seen her only for one day. But I've known her for years, and my heart has been squeezed dry of all feelings. All the care I have lavished on her has been in vain. There was a time when I eagerly looked forward to her homecoming, and now I wait anxiously for her to depart."

She looked at me uncertainly, got up to go, but stopped suddenly. "Ravi, this will lead you nowhere." Her voice was stern with warning. "There's no use pining for a derelict on whom all doors are closed."

That day I did not understand my aunt. I wouldn't even if I wanted to.

The next day I roamed about like a lost soul. I raced the horse to Lariakanta, and back to the Band Stand. When I turned homewards, I found that I was bound for elsewhere. I stood at the ridge thinking. In the afternoon, when I descended the slope to Tallital, I was clear in my mind about my destination. I had to go to Bhowali.

I got out of the bus. At the Ramgarh bus-stand, I saw heaps of luscious red apples and I knew I was not far from Bhowali. While in the bus, I had imagined it would be a small congested place. But here the tall pines swayed in the breeze and the place was drenched in sunshine. Bhowali looked beautiful. Passing through the square I came to the post office, and obtained her address. The way to 'The Pines' lay through a small bazaar. A narrow path at the turning of the main road took off towards a small hill. I looked down from the railing. Between the hills lay a small valley, criss-crossed with small fields like piece of patch-work. Far off, towards the south, a lake shone like a sheet of silver.

After this, my first visit, I came to Bhowali times without number. But not like this. This visit was different, utterly different. I walked on unthinkingly; unaware that I was going to Manno. I just walked on, that's all I was aware of. 'The Pines' was boldly etched into the trunk of a tree. I pushed open the wicket gate. Walking between two rows of flower-pots, I came to the verandah and treading softly across the carpet, I knocked gently. A bent man with a shrewd face answered the door.

"Anybody in?"

"Son, are you looking for the child?"

I nodded in reply.

"The child has gone to the lake. She should be back soon."

I sat down in the open and waited. After a while I turned my back towards the gate. When you pretend it is getting late the moments of waiting seem shortened.

The sound of horse-hoofs. I forced myself not to look back.

"Baba," someone called. I felt two eyes upon my back. I got up! Of course I knew it could be none else than Manno. There was no surprise, no eagerness in her eyes. Nor were they sad. They were just two eyes, very much like Manno's, looking at me steadfastly.

"Baba!"

The old servant came towards the horse in swift strides and said in a caressing voice, "Child, get down. It's already late." He held out his hand to help her dismount. Manno said. "Please call Amma. I'm not feeling well."

"I hope there's nothing wrong, child."

She gave a little laugh on seeing his anxious look. "Please tell Amma to prepare my bed."

The servant pulled up a chair for her. "Want to lie down?" he anxiously asked her.

"Yes, Baba."

She avoided the servant's eyes as if she was guilty of some indiscretion. Then she bent towards me. "Have I kept you waiting long?"

"Oh, no." I shook my head. "Are you unwell?"

In reply, Manno closed her eyes.

The old maidservant came running with a shawl and wrapped it round her shoulders. "Khayali, that old man is put out by trifles. You'll come around in a moment. May I bring something for the gentleman?"

Manno did not know what to say, "Amma, ask him yourself. He may not like the idea."

Her meaning was lost on me. I protested not to bother about me. Manno did not seem to have heard. Nor did she look at me.

"How is aunty?" she asked after a pause. "Is uncle still away?"

The maidservant now knew who I was. "You should have informed us about your coming. I would have asked you to bring a few things for Manno."

"Amma, please make the bed. I'm tired. I can't sit any longer."

I sat on looking a fool. How thoughtless of me. I should have at least brought some fruit for her.

Manno seemed to have read my mind. "It wasn't necessary," she said as if musing to herself. "It's not proper to bring anything or take anything from here."

I cursed myself for being so naive. I followed her into the cottage. Amma put her to bed, loosened her forehead. She pushed a chair towards me and left the room.

"Manno!"

Without speaking, she stretched her thin arm towards me and then suddenly withdrew it. Today when I am myself reduced to Manno's state, I would make a thousand sacrifices to win back that hour. While sitting there why didn't I hold her hand? As if some mysterious force had held back the flood. I sat glued to the chair, motionless.

Why this hesitation? It must have been the same fear which now keeps away my near and dear ones from me. That night when I got up to leave her room, love and fear waged a grim struggle within me. When I reached the dak bungalow, I felt a great sense of release from a bond whose every oppressive moment had held me in its shackles. I wish Manno were alive today to see the fruits of that liberation.

I had a fitful sleep. Each time I woke, I felt I was still in Bhowali, in that room at 'The Pines', with its large windows. I was lying in Manno's bed, and, sitting by the bedside, Manno was gazing at me. I stretched out my hand. Manno laughed and shook her head. "Tuck it under the rug. Who would care to touch it?"

After this phantasmagoric night when I woke again, I saw my aunt. "Ravi, it will lead you nowhere."

In the afternoon, I met uncle. He had returned the previous day, and as always he wore a grave expression. I caught his expression when he raised his eyes from the plate. I had no doubt in my mind, uncle and Manno's father must have been brothers. His eyes had the same tranquility and steadiness as Manno's.

Getting up from the dining table, uncle said, "Ravi, your aunty wants to go to Lucknow. Do you mind going with her?"

"Uncle, I'll accompany her."

My aunt, children and I were coming down from Nainital. As the bus took a turn down the broad hill road, I saw Bhowali shrouded in a haze. The same Bhowali I had visited yesterday. And then onto Kathgodam and Lucknow.

After a day's stay at aunt's place when I went to take leave of her, she insisted on my staying with her for a few days more. She was not prepared to take a no from me, it seemed. But I was adamant. "But where will you go?" she asked at last.

"I don't know," I said.

Something seemed to be weighing on my aunt's mind. "But your uncle wants you to go back to Naini."

"No, aunty, I will go south, to father."

"You will not like it there this time."

"I don't know."

At the time of parting, I touched aunt's feet. Aunt is not much older than myself. But I felt I was in need of her blessings.

She was taken by surprise. "Ravi, you have touched my feet," she said smiling. "I'll bless you for it. May you get a beautiful wife."

She had said this half in jest, and when I stood glum, she felt embarrassed.

After buying my ticket, I left the luggage with the coolie and began to stroll on the platform. There was no train in the yard. The straight railway line stretching into the distance, seemed to have uncoiled the skein of my tangled thoughts. I kept thinking, not about Bhowali. 'The Pines' and Manno but of the blessings of my aunt. A cosy home, a beautiful wife and I, around whom a dream-world revolved.

My aunt's prophecy came true. I did set up a home, and marry a beautiful girl. That is a different story though. But the train did not take me to the destination I was bound for.

The train steamed in and the coolie found a seat for me and put in my luggage while I stood outside watching the rushing crowd – passengers, coolies, women, children, old men.

"Saheb, the train will leave in a minute."

I looked at my watch and nodded my head. Adjusting his turban, the coolie said, "Saheb, don't you see? The green light is on." I looked at the green signal. And then everything swam out of focus...the same bright, thin figure, the same pallor on the face....

"Coolie, take down my luggage!"

"Saheb!"

"Hurry up, quick!"

The coolie was again following me with my luggage. I returned the ticket and purchased a new one. I bought baskets of fruit, gulped some tea, and took the train for Bareilly. I would go where I liked. Who was there to stop me – and why?

In the afternoon I sat basking on the front lawn under the winter sun. Mother came from inside and sat down by my side. "Now that you have come on leave, you should not be in a hurry to go. Why be so stubborn?"

I smiled like the wise prodigal son. Contrary to her expectation, I said, "Mother, any girl who is acceptable to you is acceptable to me."

"Son, would you like to see the girl then?"

"Yes, mother."

I felt mother was smiling to herself.

After dinner when I returned from a stroll, the room was quiet.

I started dozing while reading in bed. I dreamed I was working my way up a hill. I saw a thick cluster of pines. The sky was empty. A voice resounded in the stillness of the night and then a trembling hand groped towards my neck. The same feeble wrist, the same thin trembling fingers. I woke up with a start. My brow was damp with fear. I parted the window curtain. The lawn lay covered with light filtering from father's room.

Why was I reminded of this hand that night, a hand that I had almost forgotten, and had seen for the last time, many years ago while coming down from 'The Pines'? During a month's stay in the hills during which I had been shuttling between Naini and Bhowali, I had one day decided to cast the final die. Three times I had come down and three times I had retraced my steps while halfway.

Manno, a shawl thrown over her shoulders, was reclining in ah easy chair. I was standing by her side. "Tomorrow I will be gone from Naini," I said, breaking the ice.

Manno slowly gathered the shawl which had slipped from her shoulders. The far-off expression, which I had seen on her face a month ago, had again returned.

I wanted to say something. But what should I say? Should I tell her that I would soon return?

Every passing moment confirmed my resolve to return. But the way she looked at me suggested that I was going away forever.

"Manno..." I said.

For a fleeting moment her face became taut and then it was suffused with a faint smile. She joined her hands in farewell.

I stood rooted to the ground speechless, looking at those folded hands.

"You are getting late, Ravi."

I lowered my eyes and without a word of parting, hurried down. Would I return again, or was it the final parting?

I looked back and stopped for a moment. Manno was sitting in the same posture, like a statue.

Perhaps she had a hunch that I would turn back. "Please sit down," she pointed towards a chair. There was no anguish in her voice, nor any sign of surprise. She looked at me questioningly as if she knew I had something on my mind.

"I don't feel like going," I said with the simplicity of a child.

I looked at her, tense with expectancy. Oh, how excruciating her silence was.

She wanted to say something, as I could see. But words seemed to have stuck in her throat. "But you'll have to leave sooner or later," she said at last.

I was overwhelmed. I could have touched the very timbre of her voice with my hand.

I stepped towards her. As if to arrest the outpouring of my heart, she raised her feeble hand. "Please don't," she said. Beyond this fateful 'don't' stretched a vast emptiness.

Then she raised her thin hand in a gesture of farewell. Feeling empty and helpless, I took my way down 'The Pines'. My eyes had become misty. I looked back, bewildered. I was again standing on the bank of the lake and Manno was drifting by in a boat. She had not seen me. Her bowed head was hidden by her uplifted hand. Pohaps her eyes were closed. Or maybe she was weeping. Oh, what wounded pride! The spell broke.

I ran towards 'The Pines' but stopped at the gate.

I heard her sobbing inside.

Then I ran towards the road, increasing the distance between me and the cottage, the inmate of the cottage and those two eyes. But I could not blot out her memory. Even today the thought is fresh in my mind. I vividly recall that afternoon when Manno and

I went for a walk along the big lake. The afternoon was drenched in mild sunshine, golden and glorious. I was carried away by the pallor of her face. Her shoulders, covered with a shawl, in spite of the tired gait, were proudly erect.

When we came to the end of our promenade, we sighted two small temples under a giant tree. Their tin doors were closed. Manno stood thinking for a moment, and then taking off her shoes, she stepped over the rocks and plucked a lotus from the temple pond. She covered her head with her shawl and placing the lotus in front of the closed door, she bowed her head in worship.

When she got up, she looked strangely different, as if she was not Manno but an incarnation of her own helplessness, which had bowed its head before the closed door of its destiny.

I was touched by the melancholy exhibition of her loneliness. "I'll look around for the priest and have the temple door opened," I said.

"No, Ravi, there is no need for it," she said shaking her head. "I've no blessings to ask for. All doors are now closed on me. May these doors remain open for those who have cast me aside."

Casting to the winds the fear of catching infection from her disease which stood in my way, I bent over her head, "Manno..."

She gently pushed my hand from her shoulders. "Ravi, don't pine for what is beyond redemption."

The house was full of gaiety. Mother had got a bride after her own heart and a life companion. When I looked at Meera's innocent face, I completely lost my head. A throng of relatives and friends

– it gladdened my heart to see the house of marriage ringing with laughter. We went on a month's honeymoon to the seaside, and then to my job where we set up a new home together. My life had found its equilibrium.

And then, ten years passed. Oblivious of the impending doom, we were absorbed in each other. Torn away from Meera and the children, when lying in the cottage, I recall those days. I feel as if I still hear somebody breathing by my side. I wish I could peep into someone's eyes and tell her how happy we were then. But now there is no one at hand to listen to me. Because of the children, Meera has become cold towards me.

Last month, while going to Ranikhet, Meera had dropped in for an hour with the children. Lying in bed I saw the three of them coming up. For a brief moment she had paused at the wicket-gate. Then she had gathered the children and led them up.

"Rani, Munna, bow to your father, children!" They raised their hands awkwardly at their mother's bidding and then looked at me with curiosity. Their own father was a stranger to them.

Meera cried all the time. She was too shaken to talk coherently. For fear of infecting them, I dared not fondle my own children. I kept gazing at Meera who had come to see me. I tried to search the wife in this woman, whom I had once called my own.

I was hurt by the heartlessness of Meera looking at her wristwatch with tear-filled eyes.

Abstractedly, I stared at the wicket-gate through which my own family would presently pass, leaving me alone to my fate.

I had come to Lucknow on tour and visited my aunt. We sat chatting when my aunt's tone suddenly changed. "Ravi, do you know, Manno is no more in this world?"

I was stunned. But hiding my feelings I put on a grave expression befitting the role of a newlymade father.

"Yes, she passed away in sleep." My aunt looked at me as though I was still the Ravi of those bygone years. "The maidservant was on leave. When Khayali, the old servant, came in the morning, there was no life in her."

My aunt paused. "Ravi, you should have written to her once at least," she said wiping her tears.

"And she had left a packet for you," my aunt added. "It contained a woollen jersey."

When I returned from Lucknow, her memory kept haunting me for many days. I saw her sitting in 'The Pines', knitting a jersey for me. And I wondered why providence had doled her out a love which could not be requited.

After lying in bed for a year, I found myself in Bhowali. It was the same Bhowali with its mild sunshine and its cold wind rushing through the pines. Yes, I was here again. But this time I did not have to call at the post office to find someone's address. The first time I moved into the accursed cottage located on the hill facing 'The Pines' I wept bitterly. Had Manno been alive, she would have suffered me gladly.

Meera whom I had known for years now looks remote and alien. When my heart brims over and I pine for someone, it is of Manno I think and not Meera.

Tired of my dreary existence, when I gaze out of the window, I still see her curly hair dimly outlined in the encircling clouds.

10

Perhaps

Mannu Bhandari

Mannoo Bhandari was born in 1931 and obtained her Master's degree from the Banaras Hindu University. She is in the vanguard of women writers, having made her mark in all the three genres – literature, film and theatre. Her stories have been made into successful films. A play based on her novel, *Mahabhoj,* achieved notable success. She has a dozen collections of stories, four novels, and some books for children to her credit. Her post-Independence stories portray women in a new light.

The lights on the ship came on suddenly, breaking the dark sheet of water into fissures like a mesh with sparks caught in it. The dazzling array of electric lamps overhead, reminded Rakhal of Diwali and he wistfully looked forward to celebrating it with his family. How nice it would have been if he could come during the Pujas.

Good that he had not written to his family about his coming; he wanted to give them a surprise. The ship was scheduled to enter the docks at eight. But he got out of his uniform at six and came up to the deck. The prospect of bidding goodbye to the infernal engine room for two long months sent a surge of joy through him.

The picture of his house slid before his eyes. A long, low room built over a garage. By the time he reached home his children would be asleep and Mala, his wife, would be finishing the last chores of the evening. All her letters began with the same sentence: "I am late in writing because I had no respite from work." And then the inevitable last lines: "I must stop now. There's a huge lot of work awaiting my attention." In between, the sheet of paper was hastily scribbled over with endless recital of domestic problems, rising costs and innuendoes about the children going astray. Her letters bored Rakhal.

In the beginning, when Rakhal first joined the ship, he used to read every letter from Mala many times over. But that was ten years ago and now time had taken away some of his fervour. Even so, the prospect of being with his family once again sent a tremor through his heart.

When he was changing in the engine room, his shipmates, in their bluff, crude way poked fun at him: "You, skunk, why are you going up? To fill your lungs with fresh air? To build up your virility? Hurry up, sala! Otherwise you'll cut a sorry figure in bed."

They twitted Rakhal for sending a major portion of his salary home. He was a fool to throw away his good money on a woman, they said. But when Mala's letters came, they gathered round him and read the letters with avid interest. Even her most prosaic letters, churning out domestic inanities were so reassuring to Rakhal.

He recalled that last time, eight months after his return from leave, his wife had given birth to a daughter, Bulbul, who lived for only ten months. At her birth, Mala had written him an accusing letter. "Chhotu is only one and a quarter years old and now another baby has arrived." And when the child died, her letter conveying the sad news was again couched in the same tone: "*Hai*, why didn't death carry me away in her stead," she lamented. "She was a gem of a child, the most beautiful of all my children."

Rakhal had neither gloated over the child's arrival nor grieved over the news of her passing away. Rather, he derived some satisfaction that it was all over now. Otherwise, Mala would have spoiled his leave, lamenting, day and night, over the girl's untimely death. Soon the shore lights drew nearer and the ship dropped anchor. Taking leave of his friends and officers, Rakhal hurriedly got into a taxi. For one who had remained cooped up in the engine room on the long voyage, the vast expanse of Calcutta with its brightly-lit roads was so bracing. Racing along Lansdown Road, the taxi turned into a narrow lane and stopped in front of the fourth house. Getting out, he looked at his nondescript, squat house, built over the garage. A dim light was filtering through its only window. The sound of the taxi did not cause any stir in the house. Only a torso was momentarily framed in the window of the opposite house and was gone.

In response to his call, Mala came down hurrying. She stood looking at Rakhal for an instant and then her face lit up with joy. "Is it you? No news! No letter!"

She grabbed the hold-all from Rakhal's hand. Rakhal lifted up the two boxes and made for the dark, narrow staircase while Mala followed him lugging the hold-all, laboriously. On the stairs, Rakhal put down one of the boxes and squeezed Mala's hand. "Be careful," she said, stepping away from him. "I may drop the hold-all."

Entering the room, Mala switched on the tube-light. In its glare, the fourteen feet long room suddenly crept out of the shadows and the contours of the three children sleeping on patched up mattresses leapt into the light. There were dark circles on Mala's cheeks and streaks of white in her dishevelled hair. A window curtain, made from an old sari had slipped to one side and was flapping in the breeze.

"Why didn't you tell us in advance?" she asked. "We would have gone to the docks to receive you." She was so overwhelmed that she didn't know how to express her feelings.

"Well, go and have a wash," she said after a pause. "I'll be back in a minute."

"I don't want any food," Rakhal said. But she was already out on the staircase.

The glare hurt Rakhal's eyes and he switched off the light, blotting out the naked poverty of the room. Feeling his way through the sprawling children, he sat down by the window. It was his favourite seat.

"Why have you switched off the light?" Mala said as she came into the room. Rakhal could make out her figure etched against the dark – a figure with which he was as familiar with in the dark as in the light.

"I prefer to sit in the dark," he said.'The light may disturb the children's sleep."

"Here's some milk for you," she said handing him a glass. Then she spread out his bedding, covering it with a clean bed-sheet which she had kept in reserve.

The alacrity with which she went about her job, bespoke her happiness. She kept up a patter of talk as she worked: "Even two years is unbearably long," she said, "and this time you have come after three. Oh, how we missed you at the Pujas! I couldn't even buy new clothes for the children. Dada's electric shop has started giving him good business. He had the tube-light fixed up in the room. He could have, instead, bought clothes for my children. They went about in old clothes, looking wistfully at other children." Mala's voice became strained.

Rakhal was in no mood to listen to Mala's recital of woes. She would have enough time for it during his stay. Stretching himself on the bed, he pulled her down by his side. More than her talk, he was interested in her body.

He tried to press her against him, but she wriggled out of his arms. "Please don't!" she said in a frozen voice. "You go away, but I suffer afterwards."

Rakhal held his breath, sensing what was coming next. True enough. Mala launched forth on the Bulbul episode.

"While ill, she would just lie there staring at me with patience," Mala said in a burred tone, "'Ma, save me, Ma,' she seemed to be entreating all the time. But nothing could save her." Mala burst out crying.

Rakhal's body went cold. It angered him that she was more concerned about the departed one than about him who had come to her on leave after three years.

When he woke up in the morning, the room was filled with sunlight and looked less squalid than last night. He yawned and lighted a cigarette. As before, there was a picture of the goddess Durga hanging on the wall, thinly splashed with sandal and *rolli* marks, reminiscent of the recent Puja. By the side of the picture was a brown square mark, which reminded Rakhal that his own photograph used to be there. He looked around. The room was devoid of any furniture, except a wooden almirah with glass doors in which were lying a few knick-knacks collected from abroad during his various sojourns. His photograph was also lying in the almirah. Its frame had cracked.

Just then Reena peeped in, and finding him awake, stood awkwardly before him.

"Come here, child," Rakhal said, spreading out his arms. Reena was his pet child. But she just stood there smiling diffidently.

In three years, she had grown a lot. The incipient swell of her body under her neck made him thoughtful.

Reena ran down and after a while Bachchu came up and perched himself on Rakhal's lap. Soon Mala appeared with the tea things neatly arranged on a tray, followed by Reena carding the four-year-old Chotu across her hip. Rakhal sensed that they had all been waiting for him to wake up.

Last night's stodgy, dirty-faced children looked spruced up in home-washed clothes, There was kajal in Chotu's eyes and a thick line of sindur in Mala's parting of the hair. Rakhal was pleased. He was indeed being pampered like a VIP, the master of the house.

He wanted to take Chotu in his arms but he hid behind his mother. Last time when he came home, the boy was only one year old and he used to bounce him on his stomach.

"In a day or two, when he comes to know you, he'll not let you alone for a minute," Mala said deferisively. "Since morning he has been talking parrot-like, 'What has Papa brought for me?'"

Rakhal opened his box and started taking out the presents. The three children gathered round the box.

"This is for you," he said, handing Mala a small box.

Mala opened the box. Inside lay a tiny wrist watch. "What will I do with a watch at my age?" she said. "I'll keep it for Reena."

The children scampered off with their presents. Then suddenly Rakhal saw Shanker framed in the door. A self-deprecatory smile on his face, his lips and teeth were a shade darker than before with constant paan-chewing.

"Namaskar, Dada," Shanker said in a hearty voice.

Somehow Rakhal had never liked the man. "How are you?" he said in a cold voice.

"I'm all right, by your grace," Shanker replied.

"Have some tea, Shanker," Mala said.

"Only tea?" Shanker said baring his stained teeth to the full. "Today it must be something special. You must regale me with sweets." Then he turned to Rakhal. "Dada, this time you have come after a gap of three years. *Baudi* had a hard time of it. Of course, you never saw Bulbul. Oh, how Baudi suffered for her! She has aged prematurely."

Rakhal cast a sharp glance at Shanker. The rascal! How was he concerned with Mala's age?

"Shanker was a great help," Mala said. "But for him... Well, you know how indifferent people are these days."

Shanker was wearing a terylene shirt. Rakhal's eyes suddenly travelled to his own foreign made shirt, hanging on a peg. He pulled the shirt off the peg and put it on. Then he took a packet of cigarettes from its pocket. "Try one of these," he said holding out the packet before Shanker. "They taste different."

"This time we must pay back Shanker's money," Mala said, collecting the tea cups. "Even after scraping and scrounging, I can't manage to pay him more than ten rupees a month. It's nice of him that he doesn't mind."

Rakhal was incensed at Mala's untimely remark. She had humiliated him before Shanker. He picked up his towel and went into the bathroom.

When he returned, he saw that a new table fan was resting on a stool. Evidently, Shanker had sent it at Mala's behest.

He lit a cigarette and sat down by the window.

Shanker's garage, which was adjacent to Mr Kapur's house, had gained in dimension since he last saw it. Many cars were parked there, awaiting repairs. Shanker appeared from behind a car with Chotu perched on his shoulder. Rakhal recalled that three years ago, when he came on leave, he used to carry Chotu on his shoulder in the same manner. He felt as if the house had started rocking.

Having nothing to do, Rakhal finished his cigarette and went down to the kitchen at the back of the garage.

"Why have you come here in this stifling heat?" Mala said. "Go up and rest. The ship's food has ruined your health. You look so thin."

But Rakhal did not go. He spread a mat on the kitchen floor and sat down. He suddenly recalled that in the past when he came home on leave, Mala would not let him out of her sight.

The lunch over, Mala asked the children to go to their Uncle's house and tell him that their father had come. "And look, don't come back in this blazing sun," she said. "We'll come and pick you up in the evening." Then Mala went down to clean the utensils.

Rakhal closed the window and spreading a mat lay down to rest. Perhaps Mala had purposely asked the children to stay back at their uncle's.

The desire to be with Mala which he had felt with such keenness in the taxi last evening again took possession of him.

But Mala gave no indication of coming up. And then, to his chagrin, he heard a feminine voice talking to her.

Soon Mala came up.

"Pishima is in the kitchen," she said wiping her grimy hands on the end of her sari. "She is coming up to see you."

"Pishima? Who's Pishima?" Rakhal asked testily.

Before Mala could explain, he found an aged widow standing at the door. *"Namaskar, Jamai Babu!"* the woman said folding her hands in salutation.

"Perhaps you don't know Pishima," Mala said enthusiastically. "But for her, my children would have starved during Bulbul's illness. Pishima cooked for them for six months and also helped me in looking after the house. She's like a mother to me."

The old woman beamed at Mala's fulsome praise and then retraced her steps. Rakhal felt relieved and again lay down on the mat. Bless her soul, she seemed to be a woman of understanding.

"Why have you shut the window?" Mala asked. "Don't you feel stifled? You haven't even switched on the fan." She flung open the window.

"Shut the window, will you?" Rakhal said with an edge in his voice. "I can't stand the glare."

Mala shut the window and set the fan going. "Shanker has sent this fan for you," she said, sitting down by his side. "How thoughtful of him."

Without giving him a chance to speak, she droned on: "When you return from Dada's house in the evening, please do call on Kapur Sahib. He's fabulously rich. But there's not a trace of pride in him. Such people are rare these days. And look, do you mind, if I make small presents to his children from the things you have brought? Of course, such presents mean nothing to them. But a gesture is a gesture. And please tell me how much money you have brought with you. I still owe Shanker three hundred rupees. Bulbul's ten months' illness has left me utterly decrepit." Stifling a sob, she suddenly trailed into silence.

Had she nothing else to talk about? Shanker, Kapur Saheb, Pishima – he seemed to have no place in her small world. Why didn't she realise that he couldn't do anything about her privations? He wished he were a piece of blotting paper to soak up all her complaints!

In the evening they called on Mala's brother. "Welcome, Rakhal," Dada said hugging him. "This time you've showed up after full three years. But how thin you look! It must be the ship's food. And the salty sea breeze – it corrodes the bones!"

"Damn it! Not the salty tang of the sea, but those wretched months that I spent at your house during my period of unemployment. That's what corroded my bone!" Rakhal wanted to say. But he just twisted his lips in a grimace and then held his peace.

Dada's three children came bouncing into the room.

"Look, how eager they are to find out what uncle has brought for them!" Dada's wife said. "You've just stepped in and here they are to claim their toll tax!" she started laughing at her own joke.

Rakhal shoved his hand into his pocket and brought out two pieces of hair ribbons, and two combs which he gave to each of the two girls. And then he gave a cheap pen to the boy.

Dada's wife was disappointed. She took it out on Rakhal by offering him two pieces of Sandesh on a plate and a cup of tea. Just that and nothing more. Bachchu and Reena who were playing outside didn't even get those. As they came in, they tried to make out from the remnants on the plate as to what their father had gorged himself on.

"The cads!" Rakhal silently gritted his teeth. He would have to make up by buying sweets for the children from the bazaar.

The children again went out to play in the courtyard. Rakhal noticed that Bachchu was walking with a limp in the right leg. He had not noticed this defect before.

"Bachchu, can't you walk straight?" Rakhal shouted to the boy from where he sat. Bachchu suddenly stopped in his tracks.

"How you goat him!" Dada's wife said in a sarcastic tone. "Why blame him? He was laid up in bed for four months with a fractured leg." Then she heaved a deep sigh. "Oh, what a terrible time Mala passed through recently. Poor Bulbul, alas, she's gone for ever." She wiped away an imaginary tear with the *anchal* of her sari.

When did Bachchu break his leg? Rakhal mentally ran over Mala's letters. No, his memory was not playing tricks with him. She had never alluded to this incident in any of her letters.

"Why didn't you inform me about Bachchu's fracture?" Rakhal said to Mala indignantly as they came out of Dada's house.

"What was the use?" Mala replied in a staid voice. "You would have only worried."

A lot of things had happened in his absence. Bulbul was born and died. Reena was fast growing into womanhood. Bachchu's leg broke and was mended. Chotu had grown out of his swaddling clothes and refused to recognise him. And Mala...?

On the way home from Dada's house, he stopped in Deshpriya Park and without their asking, bought an anna worth of parched rice for each of the children. As they sat together on a bench munching at the delicacy, Rakhal questioned them about their studies.

"This oaf spends the whole day loafing about," Mala said pointing towards Bachchu. "He was laid up in bed for four months and has become a dud at studies. But he doesn't care. He has no time from play."

Rakhal knew Mala's cantankerous nature; she was in the habit of picking holes in everything, which always annoyed Rakhal, leading to further bickerings. But that evening when he returned home, after spending two hours in the park, he was feeling light at heart. The packet with the red triangle bought on the sly from the chemist's shop was safe in his pocket. He felt reassured.

The room was squalid as before. But now it looked more inviting to him. When he let go of Mala, she lay panting, drenched in perspiration and soon started snoring. The room was no longer so many square feet of space but very much a home. Rakhal lighted a cigarette and sat smoking by the window. Then sleep overcame him.

In the morning, Rakhal decided to give the room a face-lift.

Mala tried to stop him, telling him that this was a woman's job. But when he started dusting and moving the things about, she decided to lend him a hand. The room could do with a few more things. But he did not have enough money for it. Anyway, he would not be stingy with the children. He would take them on an outing, show them a picture and feed them in a restaurant. Let them realise that their father was a somebody.

"Listen," Mala said sitting in front of the fan, after she had finished her chores. "Pishima has a nephew. He has passed his Intermediate and is now working in a factory. In the evening he studies for his B.A."

Rakhal could not make out what she was driving at.

"For a long time Pishima has been asking for Reena's hand for him. Theirs is a small family, Another good thing – they won't demand a big dowry."

Rakhal got a jolt. "Are you in your senses?" he said flaring up. "Reena is too young for marriage. Don't you want her to complete her education?"

"What do you mean young?" Mala replied. "She's going on to be thirteen. I'm not asking you to marry her off tomorrow. But we must keep a boy in view. At the minimum, her wedding will cost three thousand rupees. I'm worried to death wondering where'll so much money come from."

Rakhal didn't know either.

"Did you call for me, Rakhal Dada?" Shanker stood there sucking his juice-stained tip.

Rakhal was busy shaving. "Sit down, Shanker," he said, briskly working the lather into his chin.

"Ah! you've changed the very shape of the room," Shanker looked around. "I can see your deft touch everywhere. They'll know that the master of the house has arrived." He chuckled. But this time his laughter did not jar on Rakhal.

"Mala said something about money." Rakhal wiped his face with a dirty towel. "Had I known earlier, I would have arranged for the whole amount." There was authority in his voice. Hadn't Shanker said a moment ago that he was the master of the house?

"Arre Dada Babu, where's the hurry? My money is safe with you."

"No, Shanker. A debt is a debt." Rakhal opened a small box and taking out a hundred-rupee note handed it to Shanker.

Shanker pocketed the note and went away. Rakhal counted the remaining money. Eighty rupees. When he gets his next month's salary, the bulk of it he would have to give to Mala to run the house. A big chunk would be gone on the children's entertainment. And then the end of his leave. He would go away empty-handed.

Suddenly Ranju's words echoed in his ears: "Sailors should never marry. They sweat their guts out, night and day, tending machines, and it's their wives who reap the benefit. What's the use? We're better off, brother. We can sow wild oats at every port and no holds barred!"

Pishima's nephew was coming with his uncle. Mala had invited them despite Rakhal's opposition. She had also asked her brother to be present on the occasion.

The brother arrived much in advance of the appointed time. Clad in a white starched *kurta* and Dacca *dhoti*, he looked as if he were the master of the house and Rakhal his underling.

Mala had tidied up the room and had sent for a carpet, a few chairs and some pieces of crockery from Mr Kapur's house.

The boy came – a squat youth, extremely dark and pock-marked. Rakhal had decided that he would hold the rein of discussion and not allow Dada to monopolise the stage. But his enthusiasm, the little that he had been able to work up, suddenly ebbed away.

"Rakhal Babu, we were keen to meet you. But your visits are so few and far between," the boy's uncle made the opening gambit, while taking his seat.

There was a flicker of smile around Rakhal's lips. The fellow seemed to have a shrewd eye. He knew who wore the pants in the house.

After some small talk, the uncle again turned to Rakhal. "You've visited many countries," he said. "Don't you think our Indian culture is superior to theirs – in fact, the best?"

The question pleased Rakhal. The uncle seemed to be impressed by his foreign peregrinations. But before he could open his mouth, Dada chipped in. "Oh, no, Ganguli Babu. Don't forget, Rakhal Babu remains cooped up in the engine room all the time. Where has he the time to step off the ship and study cultures?" Then he turned to Rakhal. "Anyway, Rakhal, if you have had the opportunity to go places, did you find anything comparable to our culture?"

Rakhal sizzled with anger. What did Dada think he did on the ship? Cleaned the commodes?

Ganguli Babu, proud of the fact that even in these hard times he had managed a job for his nephew, marked his triumph by devouring one *rasogolla* after another. Dada was not the one to be outdone so easily. Equally eager to drive home the point that the girl's people were in no way inferior to the boy's, he took the challenge with great gusto and kept pace with Ganguli Babu.

"Fire away!" Rakhal scowled as one *rasogolla* after another vanished into Dada's mouth. Did he think it was a free-for-all? Didn't he remember that he had offered him only two small pieces of sandesh when he visited his house?

As soon as the uncle and his nephew departed, Rakhal announced that the boy was not at all to his liking. "Tell Pishima to terminate the negotiations forthwith," he said. He was himself surprised at the stern note in his voice.

"Rakhal, you won't get such a good boy easily," Dada protested. "Don't forget that the boy is employed. That's what really matters – not looks or complexion. Besides, he won't demand a huge dowry. Can you bear the burden of a dowry? Now come off it, let's be frank about it."

"I've told you I won't have him," Rakhal persisted. "And that's the end of it. As for the dowry, that's my concern, not yours. Did you look at the boy's face?"

"You stay away most of the time," Dada said. "It's we who face the music in your absence. How can you expect me to shoulder the burden of your family in addition to my own in such hard times?"

Dada went away seething with anger.

"Did you see how he insulted me?" Rakhal said, turning to Mala. "Are you happy now? Like brother like sister!"

Mala burst out crying.

Rakhal went out, leaving Mala weeping. He bought a betel leaf at the comer shop, and licking lime off a stick, went for a stroll in the park. By rejecting the boy, he had scored over his wife and her brother. Didn't they know who he was? Nothing could happen against his wishes.

Rakhal fixed a routine for all the members of the family.

Having worked in the ship's engine room for so long, he had forgotten that he was a B.Sc. His own life was a sorry mess. He was therefore all the more anxious that his children should make good in life. He vividly recalled that in his earlier days when he was working on a job in Calcutta and Reena was born he had decided that he would make her a doctor. And now ...!

But before he could think out a plan to ensure a happy future for his children, his leave came to an end and so did his money.

"If only we could settle Shanker's debt," Mala said, as she lay by Rakhal's side. "We still owe him two nundred rupees."

Rakhal was annoyed. She had again spoiled his mood. Why couldn't she make the last night of his stay pleasant for him? A heaviness descended over his heart.

The next day his ship was scheduled to leave at ten, but he was at the docks at eight, along with Mala and the children. After donning his uniform, he returned to the quay and stood alongside Mala and the children.

When the time for the ship's departure came, he hastily handed Chotu to Mala and made to go. Chotu cried, "Baba, Baba," and started kicking his legs. Reena averted her face and quickly wiped away the tears from her eyes. When Mala bent down to touch his feet, putting the anchal of her sari round her neck, Rakhal could not hold back his tears.

"Please take good care of your health," Mala said between sobs. "And don't forget to send Shanker's money."

The ship had started on her voyage, yet above the din and clatter of her engines and the noise of the churning waters, Rakhal could still hear the feeble crying of Chotu.

Then the docks disappeared and their place was taken up by his Lansdowne Road house: He saw that Mala had dumped the mattresses in a comer and had put the boxes back in their previous places. The table fan and the stool were no longer there, nor was his photograph on the mantelpiece. Perhaps Mala had consigned it to the almirah to save it from damage.

Shanker was standing by Mala's side, consoling her, "Why do you cry, Baudi? I'm here to look to your comfort."

None of the children was there. Reena must be at the Kapur's, talking and laughing with their daughter, Pammi. Bachchu must be out on the streets, loafing about with the street urchins. Chotu must have escaped to Shanker's garage. For all he knew, Pishima would again start visiting his house. He won't be surprised if she renewed her proposal about Ganguli Babu's nephew. They all seemed to favour this match.

Rakhal shook his head. Suddenly he felt as if had come out of a false world.

"What are you doing here, hanging over the railing?" Somebody thumped his back. Rakhal sharply turned round. Ranju stood there, laughing.

"Go down to the engine-room. That's where you belong, son," Ranju said, thumping him on the back again.

Rakhal quietly descended the stairs to the engine-room. The same machines, the same familiar smell. He seemed to have found his lost bearings.

"Mate, you shouldn't be so chummy with your family," Ranju said. "Take it from me, your guru. Our fate is tied down with these machines. Son, machines we are and to machines we belong. That's what I have been telling you all the time. Here, take this oil can and feed the machines."

Rakhal took the oil can from Ranju and with great concentration of mind, pressed the nozzle into a hole.

11

The Letter-Box

Brajeshwar Madan

Brajeshwar Madan, born in Bhopalwala near Sialkot (now in Pakistan) in 1944, has had no formal education. He wrote regularly for various Hindi magazines. His collection of stories, *The Letterbox,* won an award from the Hindi Academy, Delhi. He won the Best Film Journalist's award in 1988.

It is my day off. It also happens to be a public holiday. I am standing outside The Regal, leaning against the iron railing. It is after many days that I am seeing the big red letter-box near the railing. One day I was looking around for a letter-box as I was in a hurry to post a letter and I remember this letter-box was not here. As I lean against the railing and look at the letter-box, I wonder how it happens to be here again.

I ask a young man who I have often seen standing here, "Hadn't they shifted this letter-box from here?"

"Oh, this letter-box!" the young man gives the red pillar a surprised look. "I'm seeing it for the first time."

It is amazing how people overlook things as if they just didn't exist. Only this morning a man who lives next door said to me, "Have I seen you before?" And just think of it, I have been living in the house next to his for the past several years. I thought I must be something invisible. Maybe a letter-box. I won't be surprised if a woman, a child or a man walked past me and taking me for a letter-box dropped a letter in my pocket.

In my younger days, I used to surreptitiously read my elder brother's letters. I wondered how he had come to know about it for no one had ever seen me reading his letters. In the same manner, the girl living in my neighbourhood had come to know that I owned only three shirts – a blue shirt, a yellow one and a white one. And I had never worn these shirts together at the same time!

The letter-box's red colour hits me in the eye. I never wore a red- coloured garment. My mother sometimes wore a red sari, but my grandmother invariably wore white dresses. I would often ask myself, didn't old women have red saris? One day I had opened my grandmother's box and examined its contents. It contained nothing but white clothes. White clothes look so pure. It is a marvel how people preserved purity in those days. They kept it locked in a box.

One day, I found all the locks of our boxes in the house open. All the boxes had been swept clean. Along with other things, those people had also stolen my grandmother's purity.

That girl wore skirts of variegated colours. I feared that one day the rising wind would lift up her skirt like my grandfather's upturned umbrella. We had only one umbrella in the house. My grandfather also used it as a walking stick and never went out without it. It was a constant wonder to me that he never forgot the umbrella behind. And lo and behold, one day he forgot to take the umbrella with him and never returned. By and by I learnt that he had forgotten many other things of his behind. For instance, his pair of glasses, some silver coins and rings which were lying locked in granny's box in a halo of purity.

After that theft in our house, grandfather's pair of glasses were found lying in the lane. It completely beat me how that pair of glasses had managed to slip out of granny's box and walked down into the lane. I walked through the other lanes, with my eyes glued to the ground, hoping that I may yet be able to retrieve his other articles such as the silver coins and rings which might have walked out of our house and might be lying in some lane or the other. Even now when I return home, I come with a feeling as if the tables and the chairs have put on feet in my absence. I find them lying near the door, as if looking for an opportunity to slip out of the house.

I wonder why a letter-box is always red. Father's eyes remained bloodshot most of the time. On seeing the red light at the road-crossings I am often reminded of his eyes. Sometimes I ran into him on the road and I would find it difficult to get away from him.

That girl was fond of red roses. She often reeled off the names of flowers, leaving me wondering whether flowers really had any names.

The boy standing by my side has no pockets. It's really an enigma to me. If he buys a thing, where will he produce the money from? My mother and aunt used to keep their money somewhere in their clothes, securely tied up in knots. Every woman has a knot and she opens up only if one unties that knot. I had seen the statue of a woman, half of whose body was bare and the other half covered with a sheet of cloth, having no knot in it. It seemed the sheet of cloth may rip open any moment and slip down from her body, rendering her naked, for that woman had no hands to keep the sheet from falling and exposing her body.

I had seen this statue of Venus in the house of that girl who wore skirts. At that time I was innocent of this knotty business. It was the girl's father's conjecture that the armless statue, when her arms were intact, must have been holding apples. But why apples, why not mangoes? According to a story I had heard from granny, a queen who had remained childless had given birth to a child after eating a mango. I thought my mother must have eaten a huge lot of mangoes. Whenever a child was born in our house we would find mangoe and rosewood leaves strewn across our threshold.

I remember mother used to put heavy locks on all the almirahs in our house and it was a wonder to me how such small keys could open such big locks. I often tried to search those keys, but could never lay my hands on them.

And then I suddenly realised that I had found the key. It made me happy to think that after living in the city for a long time, I was for once remembering that house and the mango and rosewood leaves.

I decided that the first thing I would do on reaching home would be to mention them in a letter to father.

But it is quite possible that tomorrow when I go out to post that letter, I may find that this letter-box has walked away and is standing right in the middle of the road surrounded by a crowd. Or it could be a man in place of the letter-box, drenched in blood, and a few blood-smeared letters peeping from his pocket, revealing his identity.

12

Supplication

Pankaj Bishta

Pankaj Bishta, born in 1946, hails from the Kumaon hills. He has made a mark as a short story writer, and is noted for his sensitive portrayal of life. He has published five collections of short stories and four novels, all of which have attracted wide attention on publication.

That night, a hundred years record was broken. The threatening clouds had been hovering over the city for many hours like a menacing army on the prowl. There were no signs of the approaching evening; it appeared it would never come. And how beautiful an evening with wispy clouds floating in the sky can be! The horizon seen through the clouds scintillating under the setting sun looks glorious; it has the enchanting beauty of a colour transparency. It looks still more enchanting when seen from behind the city trees and the high-rise buildings that are still going up. But who has the time to see all this in this teeming city. So nobody felt any regret when the late afternoon glossed over the evening and merged straight into the night. It might have only caused the people some surprise. But anything can happen in our city and we have learnt to keep our surprises to ourselves. Perhaps we do so just to save ourselves from making a make-shift reply. Yes, it is all in the game. We don't want to trot out a platitude such as "anything goes here", or hazard a guess as to the cause of something. But if you can delve into the cause of a surprise, the whole charm is lost. Hence we keep our surprises bottled up within ourselves. Just for that moment of divine bliss which is otherwise so scarce or unavailable, like pure honey.

The devastating rains that came a hundred years ago – in 1882, to be more exact – were described in the next day's newspapers, though people had a foreboding of it from the previous afternoon itself. They feared that something was going to crash somewhere.

Sitting on a charpoy set against the window, he was luxuriating in his own idleness.

"Please shut the window," he heard his wife calling from the adjoining room-cum-kitchen.

The high wind was swaying the eucalyptus trees like drunks performing *bhangra* at a marriage. Entering through the window, the wind was teasing the stove in the adjoining room like a pack of street hoodlums. Perhaps she had already done with the vegetable and taken it off the stove. He knew his wife would call him as soon as she had put the rolled chapati on the hot iron pan. Although he was waiting for her call, yet he knew lying in bed when the first chapati would be ready. Not from its smell, but by virtue of the puffed-out chapati's capacity to change the atmospheric pressure of the room. Now he had gone beyond the stage of judging things from their smells. For years his nose had remained filled with a strange smell – something like the smell of rotting paper rising from his hands all the time. In a state of poverty, even the puffing of a chapati can tell on his nostrils. He knows the chapati is baked. The pressure is very pronounced with the first chapati, but it keeps on losing its intensity with the subsequent chapatis. The breath adjusts itself to the smell of chapatis as they come off the pan.

The dust had started ravishing the room which my wife had tidied up with such care. She would keep fulminating against it when she started dusting the room tomorrow morning. But the poet was just not concerned. He would take everything in his stride – the dust, the water, the air – and make himself scarce after seeing the house enveloped in dust.

Calling him a poet? It sounds like an abuse. He is not a poet, not by a long shot. He hasn't ever written even a line of verse.

Yes, he had perforce to read poetry in his college days and that was the end of it. If he ever wrote poetry, he did not remember it, though he would not like to make an argument of it.

Outside, the storm has gained in velocity. A strong gust of wind carries away all the papers lying on the cornice. Though of a lethargic nature, he pounces upon a piece of paper flying in the air and grabs with the exuberance of a child catching a butterfly.

He starts reading the paper. A letter from Munna. The very first sentence puts him off. He has asked his wife so many times not to preserve these letters, that she should tear them off as they arrive. But in spite of his admonitions he finds these letters all over the place. Nothing else comes in the post except Munna's letters. He would like to destroy these letters without reading them, but just the same they fascinate him like a horror movie.

"Bhai Saheb, our city is also undergoing a great change," Munna has written. "Where there were previously roads, now their place has been taken by drains and drains have changed into roads. We have given up the ground floor. We just couldn't help it. No, there was no way out: Even the dirty water does not drain out. We sometimes get in and go out through the windows. The house remains filled with stench. It just hangs in the air without our being able to decide where it comes from. Mother asserts that sewage water does not give out such powerful stench and Babuji agrees with her. According to me, the water that has been stagnating on the ground floor for so long is responsible for this stench. At this mother removes the pad of cloth from over her nose, sniffs around and exclaims, 'You are all a pack of fools! This is the smell of those rotting certificates and testimonials!'

"Bhai Saheb, could this be a cogent reason? I have smelt all my certificates and testimonials, specially the degree certificate. They are no doubt falling apart but they don't smell.

"I asked Urmila about it. 'Sister, what have you to say about it?' I asked her. She did not come out with a reply for many days, but one day when I had a squabble with father and mother over it, I couldn't hold myself back. 'Can a man remain unconcerned just like that?' I put it to her in so many words. 'This policy of indifference is insufferable.' It was only then that she spoke. 'It is not a question of policy,' she said. 'I have lost my sense of smell. I don't smell anything.'

"I am surprised. How can one lose the faculty of smelling? She was not like this before. I kept brooding over it for many days. Why was Urmila jiji so cut up about it? I kept wondering for none of us could sleep at night because of this powerful stench. And not having slept for months together we had become snooty and short-tempered and fought like cats. No, she was not telling a lie. The other day when I saw her under the first light of the morning sun, I was taken by surprise. I saw Urmila jiji's face turning solid and squat; it was so devoid of expression. No, there was not even a slight hint of expression on it. 'What's happened with you?' I asked her. 'I don't know,' she replied in a flat voice. 'Just have another look. I don't see anything wrong with my face.' But when I touched her face with my finger, I found it hard like Plaster of Paris and cold under the morning's moisture. My finger had left a mark on it as if I had touched a window-pane on a cold December morning. Bhai Saheb, can a person turn into white earth in a jiffy?'

"Babuji thinks that the dust from the disintegrating bricks of our ancestral house has settled on jiji's tender face. As a precautionary measure, he has started pasting up paper on those incriminating bricks which have begun crumbling badly."

Munna had concluded his letter by saying, "Bhai Saheb, I cannot bear this stench any longer. I want to come over to you. You need not worry about sister though. The dust has settled only up to her throat. Yesterday mother managed to land on the street with the help of a rope and purchased a talisman from a shop. This will do sister good, I hope. You know how meticulous father can be. He is taking all possible precautions."

And then there was a postscript: "If possible please send me Khub Khelo's special cricket number and a Kapil Dev blow-up."

"Are you listening?" his wife said. "Someone is knocking at the door for the last one hour!"

Wonder of wonders! What sharp ears! How could she hear the sound of knocking above the humming and hissing of the burning stove? And here he was, a good-for-nothing fellow! Cursing himself, he proceeded towards the door which opened onto the street.

"Who's there?" he cautiously enquired before opening the door.

"Me," a tired voice came from outside.

It could be Munna – the thought suddenly flashed through his mind.

But if he was coming, he wouldn't have asked for the special cricket number of Khub Khelo. Munna was a strange fellow indeed. There was a stale sameness about all his letters and they were invariably undated. How could one determine which letter came when? This letter could have been an old one. Though habitually lazy, he must make a special bid to send Munna the special number. And he did make a special effort. But every time he went there, he found that it had been sold out and he had to wait for a fresh stock. And he had to queue up every time. True, it was a democracy where all were equal. But it was nothing short of a farce to stand in a queue in front of a magazine office for endless hours for a measly special number. Besides, he was a married man.

He could not decide who could this 'me' be. He thought it rather odd to enquire again and flung open the door.

"You?" Who was it? Was it Munna? But could a man change so much beyond recognition? He was in a quandary. Had he quarrelled with someone before coming? He got unnerved on seeing the man's condition.

"I'm No. 20199843."

Why was he looking so shattered? And how he bled! In this precarious condition when his head was so seriously injured exposing the gray matter through the skull he should have gone to the hospital in the first place.

"Who are you?" he asked again, unable to recognise the man standing before him, drenched in blood.

"I'm 20199843."

"But..." he hesitated in bewilderment "But this is Munna's number," he said.

The blood was still dripping from the man's body. "No," he said with an air of finality. "This is my registration number. You had given it to me."

Suddenly the stench became more pronounced. He clenched his hands and held them at his back (perhaps mother was right after all). Yes, it was his number. Munna's number should also be somewhere close to it in the serial order.

"You will get a call letter. You had passed the typing test, I hope?"

"Do you know where my bag is?" the man bearing the number 20199843 asked.

"Bag? What bag?" he could not remember what kind of bag the man was alluding to.

"The bag, of course. It contained Rs. 1,200. For the material."

"Oh!" He just couldn't understand what the man was driving at.

"My bag! It contained eight hundred-rupee notes, three fifty-rupee notes, fifteen ten-rupee notes and the rest were five-, two- and one-rupee notes. To purchase the material."

"No, I know nothing about your bag." He shook his head gloomily.

"But you were there all right," the bleeding man said.

"Where?"

"In the morning. In the crowd."

Yes, now he remembered. His gray slightly soiled striped pants which was shining in the light of the room like a bright piece of rag reminded him of the whole thing.

His bus had suddenly stopped when he was still about two kilometres away from his office. There was a heavy traffic jam ahead of them. In the gruelling heat of May who could continue to sit in a jampacked bus at the rush hour of ten? And to make things worse, he had been strap-hanging. There were no indications of the bus resuming its journey soon. Those who were standing were the first to get down. Some who were sitting also gave up the luxury of their seats. To get over the worry of not making it to the office in time, he was going to light a cigarette when word went round that there had been an accident. A cyclist, it was said, had dashed in to a bus. The office commuters had emerged from the bowels of the buses like ants getting out of their holes into which rain water had seeped. He slowly walked up to the spot where the crowd was standing in a circle.

"He's dead!" someone said.

"No, he's still alive," another man said.

"But he is not likely to survive," a third man said.

"Has the police come?" a fourth asked.

"Don't you see who is standing in front of you?" someone from the crowd said.

"But why is the policeman standing idle?"

"He's not standing idle. He is waiting for the ambulance."

"But how will the ambulance reach here?" a man asked.

"I fear he's going to die," the man who had predicted the victim's death said.

"But they should take him away from here," a man said.

"It is not the policeman's job," a man rejoined.

"Oh, when is the traffic going to ease up?" he asked the policeman while lighting a cigarette.

"When the ambulance comes," the policeman replied.

"And when will the ambulance come?" the man asked, showing some surprise.

"Can't you see how snarled up the traffic is?" the policeman said testily, visibly annoyed. "One is already dying. Do you want one or two more to be crushed to death under the wheels of the ambulance? It is as simple as that. As soon as the traffic opens up, the ambulance will be here. Oh, one comes across such stupid fellows."

The policeman's stricture and the crowd's pervasive laughter hurt him; he felt so slighted. The general laughter had made a dent in the circle of spectators through which he could see the man's feet who was lying prostrate on the road. His feet were showing through the ends of his striped trousers. Oh, was this the same man whom he had met in the morning? But he could not come to any definite conclusion. Not to speak of the man's face, he had had only a partial glimpse of the man's feet. Moving away from the crowd, he returned to his bus. Standing under its shade, he started brooding over the fate of his country. No, his country was too far gone; its condition was now beyond redemption. He used to think of his country only when he was personally involved, when he found himself in some dire predicament. He kept brooding endlessly and in endless wait for the bus to start again. In the meanwhile the policeman had dispersed the crowd. The traffic had also started crawling forward. He quickly boarded his bus.

If the man was alluding to the morning's accident, then it must be the same man.This conviction had slowly started gaining on him. The lightning had flashed to the accompaniment of heavy thunder in which he had seen his torn trousers. It was grazed in so many places and spattered with blood.

"It's going to rain heavily," he said to himself.

"Can you tell me something about it?" the visitor who was covered with blood asked.

"But you should have received the call letter," he said.

"Your office told me that the letter was posted last winter," the visitor said.

"So?" he asked hopefully.

"But I've still to get it. Perhaps it froze somewhere on the way due to the severe cold."

"Cold? You mean the winter cold?"

The visitor was silent.

"I'll look into it," he assured the visitor.

"But unless the cold defreezes, that letter can't travel up to me. That's why I'm searching for my rupee notes. Please tell me where to find them since you were there at that time."

"But there were so many other people besides me," he said with a slight edge to his voice. "I was not the only person present there."

"I'm not asking everybody," the visitor said wearily.

"But where is the proof that you had all that money with you?" he asked.

He was getting suspicious of the man. Was he trying to fork out money from people by showing them his broken head?

"If you like I can give you some money," he said to get rid of the man, and without waiting for his answer he went in to fetch the money. How much should he give him? It had taken him a few seconds to decide. The man was really in a bad shape. He returned holding a five-rupee note in his hand.

The thunder had increased and was now coming peal upon peal. The sky looked a blinding desolation. Houses, trees, lamp-posts shook as the thunder rolled on. But the bleeding man was nowhere to be seen. Where could he have gone in that wretched condition? Looking puzzled, he advanced a few steps hoping to locate him somewhere around the place. But the man seemed to have vanished for good.

"Good riddance!" he said to himself smacking with satisfaction. A sensible man should have nothing to do with a sordid man like him having marks of blood on his person. The police could have hauled him up for nothing. It had started drizzling and the drizzle changed into a downpour as he advanced a few steps. He bolted the door and coming back to his bed, stretched himself on it. With the first wink of sleep everything came back to him. Wouldn't they have taken Number 20199843 to the hospital by now?

In the morning he was alarmed on seeing footmarks on the floor – blood-marks coming from outside and ending by the side of his charpoy.

It had been quite a job for his wife to wash these stains; she had used many buckets of water in the process. It was only when the blood-marks were wiped out that he got down from his charpoy. Lucky for his wife that he did not go to the extent of asking her to wash and scrub outside the door also. It had rained heavily last night, breaking a hundred years' record and the rain had washed the whole place clean.

That night Saxena was the shift-incharge of *The Morning Times.*

When he put the front page of the city edition to bed, no news of the new record had come on the ticker-tape either from PTI or from the UNI. Of course the news of the record could not be relayed because it was still raining. So far as the news of the rain was concerned, Saxena had devoted four columns to it under a double decker heading: Heavy Rain Lashes The City. Many Areas Under Water. After handing in the page, he went to sleep on the table. The Transport Department had informed him that the vehicles that had gone out with the men of the first shift had got stranded somewhere en route.

The rain had set a new record indeed. There had not been such heavy rainfall in the last hundred years, so the PTI had recorded the following afternoon, quoting the authority of the Meteorological Department. In May 1909, in 24 hours, it had rained 4 centimetres which was a record for that period. But on that day of May, it had rained 12 centimetres, breaking all previous records. A stupendous figure indeed!

The Morning Times had been able to do full justice to the news only in its next issue. Saxena had his weekly off that day. Even so the report had found a place on the front page in two-column space after the third day of the rains.

On the same day, on the basis of the news which the city reporter had obtained from the public relations man of the Police Department, there was a four-line report on the third page to the effect that one Kunwar Singh, aged 28, was run over by a city bus at the city crossing. The police had immediately rushed him to the hospital where he died after four hours of his admission. He had remained unemployed for many years after graduation and last year he had been advanced a loan to set himself up as a vendor of snacks. The Prime Minister had performed the inauguration ceremony of his business.

It was nowhere mentioned in the report that the number assigned to him by the Employment Department was 20199843.

He thought over the matter for some time and then sent a telegram to Munna.

13

Sargam Cola

Asghar Wajahat

Asghar Wajahat was born in 1946 and is now a name to reckon with in Hindi literature. He holds a post-doctorate in Hindi from Jawaharlal Nehru University, and is an acclaimed author in the Hindi language. With several collections of stories, novels and plays to his credit, he is best known for his incisive comments on life. He is teaching Hindi at the Jamia Milia Islamia, Delhi.

Just as the canine population gets into heat at the approach of Kartik, the eighth month of the Hindu calendar, the elite of Delhi get into a craze for art and culture at the approach of winter. Winter is also the time when the city swarms with white-skinned foreign tourists. You see them around laughing and joking and bubbling with exuberance. They are said to be the biggest buyers of our culture and are, therefore, recognised as its connoisseurs. Not far behind them are the leisured class, specially the women of high families, with their faces heavily painted like those of the glamorous women of calendar art. In winter they spend their evenings going round art exhibitions or watching plays. Winter is indeed the 'art' season of Delhi. The sun sets quite early in winter and a cold bracing wind springs up caressing the soft woollens of the people who frequent music conferences or art exhibitions, just for the pleasure of being singled out as the 'arty' people. It is the kind of winter wind, charged with sweet and heady fragrance, that can turn an impotent into a he-man and a he-man into an impotent. Satiated with the fullness of life, people get steeped in art and music and these in turn seep into them.

That evening a big music conference was in progress and a large number of VIPs had turned up. There were four policemen posted at the gate of the pandal. Bored and weary, they were lazily toying with their batons. Behind them stood two police sub-inspectors lazily watching the scene, and conscious of the fact that they had four policemen to lord over.

A gravelled path led up to the gate, apparently freshly laid for the occasion, flanked on both sides by flower pots dug into the earth, leaving it to the people to wonder how flowers could grow in such profusion in arid ground. A canopy of white paper flowers stretched over the path. Canopies of genuine flowers were to be seen in the past on the graves of pirs and faqirs. In course of time the practice caught on and they started decorating their wedding pandals with such flower canopies. The path leading to the conference gate was flanked by bamboo poles covered with coloured cloth, with bright tubelights fixed over them.

Das Gupta, who was lingering outside the gate, could not see what was going on inside the pandal. As he stood there, he wistfully watched the people going in. He did not miss the people in high heels who were making an ineffectual effort to look taller than they actually were and seemed to give the impression that the programme had been arranged exclusively for their benefit. There were middle-aged women with faces that foreign cosmetics had played havoc with. Red sari to match with red eye shadow, blue sari with blue eye shadow. They seemed to have exhausted all the colours of the rainbow over their faces. Then there were women in jeans, walking staccato on high heels, the symbol of affluence, or so Das Gupta thought. Grave faces, some sternly grave, others sterile, denoting wealth, fame, respectability, free from any taint of dejection or disappointment. The crowd passed by – hep girls with strange hair-do, boy-killing girls, and dogs shadowing them – doggies, dear doggies and more doggies.

The function had started. It was Bhimsen Joshi's voice. But Das Gupta was still cooling his heels outside the gate. He had not been able to procure a ticket to go in.

The gate, the gravelled path, the well tumed-out visitors, the police officers and their men. At some distance from the conclave, on the right side of the gate, Ajab Singh had set up his kiosk under a tree where he sold cigarettes and paan. Surprisingly, even in a big city like Delhi, Ajab Singh and Das Gupta happened to know each other. Moving away from the gate Das Gupta came up and stopped before Ajab Singh's kiosk. The cold had increased and Ajab Singh had started a fire in a wrought iron pan.

"Ten biris."

'That makes it thirty, Dada."

"Yes, that makes it thirty. When did I say it does not add up to that figure? I'll certainly pay you up." Das Gupta took the bins from Ajab Singh. He lighted one from the fire in the pan and took a long pull at it.

"You've hot been able to manage it, Dada?"

"Oh, yes, I will. I'll, surely."

"Better go home. It is going on to be eleven."

"No, not to that blasted home of mine. I want to hear Bhimsen."

"Two single Banarsi (paans)."

A note of Bhimsen Joshi's music came floating outside the pandal.

"Wills."

"No, not these. King size."

Das Gupta moved away from the kiosk, hoping that he would be able to hear the music more clearly by getting closer to the gate. But the sound had drifted away and then stopped. He had a brain-wave. Why not steal into the pandal by the backside? Taking a long pull at the biri, he came to the backside of the pandal. Darkness, trees. He leapt forward. A light flashed on him.

"Who's there, eh?" Who could speak so curtly except a policeman?

Das Gupta quickly opened the buttons of his pants. "I've come to make water," he said. 'To piss, you know."

The torch went out. Das Gupta felt like pissing on the policeman. These salas, how duty-conscious they could be at a time when it was least called for! The urine sprayed the policeman in a thick stream. It also fell over the pandal, drenching the audience. The morons, yes, how else to describe them? They rushed out of the pandal in panic.... Das Gupta started laughing.

Throwing away his biri, he returned to the kiosk. They had improvised a make-shift canteen near the kiosk. A counter made by putting two tables together, a coffee plant, a two-hundred-watt electric bulb hanging over it. Hot dogs, hamburgers, pop corn, coffee cups, plates.... Das Gupta attuned his ears to catch the strains of music wafting from the pandal. It was meant for the people inside the pandal. And the bloody fool who could appreciate the music was standing outside the pandal making a complete ass of himself. The loud-speaker those scoundrels had put up inside the pandal hardly carried the voice outside. He had to strain his ears to catch the sound. And those inside the pandal were complete duds, having no ear for music. Did they really understand Bhimsen Joshi? Could they understand the subtlety of the maestro's notes? If one were to explain to them that the maestro could sing on the entire scale, from low notes to the medium and then on to the high notes, making a magical bridge of sounds in one breath, they would feel so befuddled that they would flee from the pandal. Didn't Bhimsen Joshi know what kind of audience he was trying to regale with his music? Surely, he must be knowing. Oh, what pretence! They made a bee-line to the pandal as if they were great connoisseurs of classical music. And within ten minutes of their arrival, they became restive, finding one excuse or the other to quit. They would go somewhere and eat and eat and eat, and having stuffed their bellies, they would go to sleep.

"Dada, it's gelling chilly." While making a paan, Ajab Singh's fingers were becoming stiff with cold.

"It shouldn't cause you any surprise. It's the month of December."

"Take a brick, Dada. A brick." Ajab Singh picked up a brick from the wayside and offered it to Das Gupta to sit on it.

As the night advanced, and the stillness increased, the voice coming from within the pandal became clearer. The Ustad was going to start on a khayal. Das Gupta shifting on his small seat of the brick became more attentive... *pag lagan de... dhi-dhi... dhage tirikit tu na katta dhage ... tirikit dhi ni.* "Who's accompanying him on the tabla?" Das Gupta asked himself. Oh, how well he performed!

"Who's performing on the tabla?" he asked Ajab Singh.

"I don't know, Dada," Ajab Singh laughed.

"What virtuosity! What dexterity! The sound keeps descending into the very depths of your being ... *tu na katta ...*"

"*Tumhare pas* Campa *hai*? Do you have Campa?"

They were three girls and four boys. Two girls were in jeans and they had long hair falling to their waists. The hair of the third girl was short and did not cover her ears. One of the boys was wearing a leather jacket while the other two were in Assamese jackets. The fourth had a black blanket thrown round his shoulders. His trouser legs were so narrow that his spindly legs grotesquely stretched out in them. One of the girls with long hair kept tossing it back though there was no need to. The third girl kept fingering her nosering.

"Have you got Campa?" the boy with the spindly legs asked in a pronounced British accent.

"No, we have just run out of it."

"Oh, how silly," the girl with short hair grumbled.

"What a stupid canteen they have."

"We must complain."

"Sweeties, let's have coffee," the boy with the long legs said airily. "But I can't have coffee here," the girl wearing the nosering siad. She was more beautiful than all the other girls.

"W-h-y, my dear?" the boy with long legs hesitated for a moment. The other girls looked annoyed.

"I always have coffee at home or at the Oberois."

"Fine. Let's go to the Oberois then," the boy with long legs said in a loud drawl.

"Sir, sir, Campa is here!" the bearer of the canteen said pointing his fingers at a man who was coming towards them with a crate of Campas on his head.

"Oh, Campa has come!" the girls exclaimed in chorus. From within the pandal the voice of Bhimsen Joshi floated out.

"Oh, Campa-a-a has c-o-m-e!" they all sang with one voice. "C-a-m-p- a.... *Par karo ... Araj suno ... o o o ... Par ...* C-a-m-p-a ... *Par karo ...*"

"But now I want to have coffee at the Oberois," the girl with the nosering drawled in a plaintive tone.

"But we have come here to listen to Bhimsen Joshi."

"Oh, don't be silly. He's going to sing the whole night Let's have coffee at the Oberois and then we can come back. We can even have some sleep. Time enough for music and all that." The long-legged boy broke away from the group, waving his key-ring. Bhimsen Joshi's voice, now saturated with sadness, was drifting our more powerfully: *"Araj suno moree ..."*

Bang! Bang! The car doors shut together and the car's engine growled in the cold.

It was past twelve. The road was steeped in silence with cars parked on both sides of it stretching into the distance. The people had started coming out of the pandal, most of them middle-aged, looking a little bored and lost in themselves, many of them accompanied by fat women, wih lumps of flesh hanging from their waists. They yawned as they proceeded in search of their parked cars. This *sali* slept. It can be so overpowering. A costly ticket gone to waste. The Ustad would get into his mood only after two and these people don't have the patience to wait till then. They asked their drivers to fetch them some tickets, sat in the pandal for an hour or so, and then decamped. What kind of audience do they make? A slur on the Ustad's fair name. How they honoured him! Their seats had fallen vacant. Why couldn't he occupy one of them? Das Gupta muttered to himself. They had already been paid for. Surely, he deserved to be given a chance.

Das Gupta started feeling chilly and he shoved his hands deeper into the pockets of his second-hand, over-sized, airforce overcoat. Ajab Singh gathered some dry leaves to keep the fire going.

The director of The Art Centre emerged from the pandal. "Sala!" Das Gupta muttered under his breath, eyeing the man malevolently. He had built a nice house by raking in profits on the poor painters' creations. And now he was dabbling in sanitary fittings business. He brazenly maintained that he had made good in life, forgetting that he had done so by cultivating the 'art' of buying votes and supplying girls. He gave with one hand and gathered with the other. Oh, how the organiser of the Music Conference ran forward to open the car door for him! The door of the imported car gently swung shut and Kusum Gupta, the organiser, turned to go. She is neither a Miss nor a Mrs., Das Gupta thought. And then an idea flashed through his mind. He knew her very distantly. Why hot approach her with a request to let him in. She was swiftly proceeding towards the entrance.

"Er ... can you please ...?" Das Gupta mumbled in English.

She did not care to hear him properly. She had understood his purpose and shrugged her shoulders.

"No, I'm sorry. We have spent thirty thousand to arrange this…." She disappeared into the pandal.

Thirty thousand, fifty thousand, one lakh. Profit, profit. She could think of nothing except making money. He came back and resumed his seat on the brick.

"Wills."

"Sweet paan." '

"Try number ninety. Ninety!"

"Oh how mean you are!" The innocent looking boy was not allowing the woman-like girl to have a go at his hamburger. The girl stretched out her hand to grab the hamburger and the boy pulled back his hand. The other two girls with them giggled.

"Mean!" the girl said tartly.

Mean? What did mean stand for? Das Gupta asked himself. Didn't it stand for a low-down person? But how sweetly these people uttered the word as if it stood for something sublime.

The innocent looking boy and the woman-like girl dug their teeth into the same hamburger. The other girls laughed as if the two were making love in their presence.

"Did you attend the Chawlas' party?"

"Oh, no. I wanted to go but ..."

"Mehras give nice parties."

"Hai Bobby!"

"Hai Litti!"

"Hai John!"

"Hai Kilty!"

"Yes, the Mehras give nice parties because they have a nice lawn. Last time their party was just terrific. There was so much to eat and drink. We came back at 2.30 in the morning. You know why we had to leave so early? My mother-in-law was there in our house.... Did you meet her? She looks so charming even at the age of seventy-three. So attractive – oh, I just can't describe her."

"Did you like the bridegroom?"

"Oh, he's so handsome."

"Did you notice the ring he was wearing?"

"Oh, yes. Beautiful."

"Must be very expensive."

"Oh, sure."

"My mother's uncle has got a similar ring."

"It's platinum."

"Hey, waiter, two coffee!"

"These skunks won't let me listen to the music," Das Gupta grumbled to himself. The music coming from inside was faintly audible. Das Gupta pushed the brick forward, bringing it nearer the fire.

"He had just come back from Europe."

"He has a house in London."

"Must be very rich."

"Of course he is. The Ustad charges ten thousand for a night."

"Then I'll call him to sing at our marriage." The innocent-looking boy put his arm around the woman-like girl's waist.

"Look at his hand, look at his wrist!" Das Gupta muttered to himself. "He can't earn a single paisa by dint of his own efforts. But he has the audacity to invite the Maestro to perform at his marriage because of his father's wealth."

Ajab Singh threw some more dry leaves over the sinking fire. A driver came smoking a biri and sat down to warm bis hands by the fire. He was wearing a Khaki lively.

"It's so cold – it's seeping into the bones," the driver said. Nobody spoke.

"Let's see how long this nonsense lasts. Driving 150 kilometres at this pace has killed me. The sala took it into his head to hear the mujra at two in this freezing cold."

"It'll continue till six in the morning," Ajab Singh volunteered the information.

"Then I'm done for," the driver said throwing up his arms.

"Brother, do you have a pass?" Ajab Singh asked the driver.

"A pass? You mean an admit card? Do you want to go in?"

"Our Dada wants to go in," Ajab Singh pointed towards Das Gupta.

"Let me see." The driver got up and swiftly proceeded towards the gate. He looked so tall and hefty, as he walked away taking long strides. A Jat from Haryana. He had a word with the policeman at the gate who accosted a receptionist.

The driver returned to Ajab Singh's kiosk taking long strides. "Oh, how cold it is! How chilly!" He held out his hand. "Here are the passes," he said. "But they are four passes."

"Doesn't the receptionist know that I am the driver of the S. P. Crime Branch North District? Have them. Have all the four of them. What good are they to me? Have I to pickle them?"

"One will do for me," Das Gupta said.

The Haryana Jat who was bored stiff by now was in no mood to prolong the issue. He tore up the remaining three passes and threw them in the fire. Then he and Ajab Singh held their hands over the leaping flames of the burning paper.

As Das Gupta proceeded towards the gate of the pandal, he could clearly hear the music emanating from within. *Ja ... go ... jago ....* The Ustad was running through *the alaap* – leading to the morning's Bhairavi. *Jago Mohan Piare ... dha dha, dhi, dha, ti, ti, ta ... Jago M-o-h-a-n ... P-i-a-r-e...*

14

The Devotee

Abdul Bismillah

Abdul Bismillah, born in 1949, in the Allahabad district teaches Hindi at the Jamia Milia Islamia, Delhi. His published works include novels, collections of stories and volumes of verses. An outstanding short story writer, he came into the limelight with his novel *Jhini Jhini Bini Chadarya* which won him the Sovietland-Nehru Award and the Kedia Award.

Pir Saheb was resting inside on a mattress while his associates were sitting outside on the verandah crowded with devotees, whom they were initiating into the various ways of intoning the holy words. They twisted their mouths into comical shapes and swayed their heads while reciting them and the devotees assiduously aped the manner of their preceptors.

My grandfather was sitting among those devotees. He had had his beard trimmed after many months and was wearing the *sherwani* which had been consigned to a box for years together. In his younger days the sherwani had formed the main item of his dress and he wore it every day. Later on, he used it on special occasions such as a festival or a feast. And now he wore it very sparingly, only when he went to make his obeisance to Pir Saheb. The sherwani had three conspicuous patches and its collar had frayed and looked like a tattered frill. He had its pockets altered and kept money in them. But that day his pocket contained only a soiled and dog-eared two-rupee note. His hand frequently felt the note as he sat there reciting the holy words.

I was sitting by his side, raptly watching him. In fact, I was feeling utterly bored, my luck not having provided me with any device to dispel the boredom I often fell a victim to. After Abba's death, I had started living with grandfather and he took me along wherever he went. Whatever the occasion, he always got embroiled in some controversy – about the country, about religion or about our community. Most of what he said went over my head. I had no interest in these discussions. Oh, it was so boring! But even so, I resolutely stuck it out with him.

Our house was all the time steeped in gloom; everything looked so bleak. After Abba's death, it had become the hotbed of squabbles. My Abba was the sole breadwinner of the family and with his passing away, our income had seriously shrunk. Grandfather was not up to much and my uncle had separated from the family. We were eking out an existence by selling our property bit by bit. Because of these financial difficulties, my mother often tried, through the good offices of my grandmother to prevail upon grandfather to let her go and live with her parents. But he would have none of it.

"If my son is gone, has that made my daughter-in-law redundant?" grandfather would argue. "She's as much a part of our family now as she was then."

This would always end in a quarrel with my grandmother. As a result, mother could neither leave the house nor have any peace of mind. Unfortunately, I could not remain aloof from these bickerings. Sometimes, being too young to understand the gravity of the situation, if I happened to make some extravagant demand, I would come in for a thrashing. After beating me, mother would keep crying for a long time. But that only added to the tension.

As compared to us, uncle was not badly off. But he never bothered to give my grandfather any monetary help. If he came to invite grandfather on Bakr-Id it would lead to a serious row.

"I denied myself every comfort to have you educated and to teach you some craft," grandfather would say. "Was it to face these wretched times? As soon as your wife came, you washed your hands off the family. You never care to find out whether this old man or the old woman is hungry or going about naked for want of clothes. And today you have come to show your affection for us? I piss on your food."

Uncle was not in the habit of taking things lying down. In reply, he would say something nasty, auntie doing her best to fan the flames. Angered, grandmother would beat her breasts and cry. The festive mood would change into a feuding tit-for-tat Amma would also start crying while I could do nothing but look on helplessly.

Then I saw a great change coming over grandfather. He read the *namaz* five times a day and never quarrelled with anyone. By the time I had left my childhood behind, he had retired from his school teacher's job. Till then, he had never said the *namaz* except on Id or some such festival. I was surprised at this sudden change.

Then he started making occasional trips to the city. Later on I learnt that he had become the devotee of a Pir Saheb.

Apart from the portion of the house that had gone to uncle, three rooms had fallen to our lot. Of these, we had rented out one room to a man of our village. We ourselves lived in the second room. The third was filled with junk – iron rods, discarded chairs and *charpoys*, tattered clothes and heaps of such other rubbish. Grandfather had made a place for himself in that room by spreading out a tattered mat in one comer. He kept an aluminium pot by the side of the mat. An old apron cloth spread on the floor served to hold the Holy Quran. His meals were sent to him in the room and he ate them without demur and then returned to his prayers and meditation. He rarely left the room – not even in summer.

Some signs of liveliness appeared on his face only when there was news that Pir Saheb had come to the city. Grandfather would immediately start making preparations to go to the city. He washed his clothes in the river and got his beard trimmed by the barber. Then, taking me along, he would set out for the city.

Generally, he didn't have any money on him. He had to ask for it from grandmother who never parted with it without a squabble.

That day too, asking me to wait, he went to grandmother to ask her for some money.

"What's it that you want?" she asked in a mocking tone.

"I want some money," grandfather tossed off the request with a casual air.

"You think I have trees that grow money?" grandmother said in a sharp voice.

"Don't be angry. Pir Saheb has come."

"So what? How am I concerned, tell me?"

"I must have something to offer to Pir Saheb."

"Where's the need?" grandmother cried. "What good does it serve your becoming a devotee? Has it lessened your worries?"

Grandfather flared up. This question was a direct attack on his convictions and faith.

"Get out of here!" he cried. "Begone, all of you. This is my house. As long as I earned, all of you blithely chewed off the meat from the bone. Not a word you uttered as if you were tongueless. Now that only the bone is left, you want to throw it away. Have I no say in this house? Your stomach churns food because of me. It's the rent of the room that keeps you going. What do you do with all that money? I want a clear account."

The last statement had, in fact, taken the force out of grandfather's argument. It was now grandmother's turn to go full tilt at him.

"What rent are you speaking of?" she cried. "Here, I'm ready to give the account of those measly twenty rupees. If I stop taking in tailoring jobs, your neck will lose its stiffness in no time."

"Yes, I must have the account," Grandfather insisted. "What have you done with those twenty rupees, tell me?"

Grandmother started reeling out the details of those expenses. It transpired that all that was left to her now was a two-rupee note which she had tied to the end of her *orhni*.

She undid the knot and threw the soiled two-rupee note in front of grandfather. Then she started crying. Grandfather picked up the note without uttering a word and put it in the pocket of his sherwani. Gesturing to me to follow him, he started for the city.

The skirmish between my grandparents made me sad. Grandmother's weeping face haunted me and I felt like crying. It set me thinking. Why did it happen like this, I asked myself. In the end, I felt that religion was at the bottom of it. If religion is for the good of the people, why do these Pirs accept money from the poor? But I could not gather courage to put this question to grandfather.

The city was about eight kilometres from our village. Walking the entire distance we arrived in the city in the evening and went to the place where the Pir Saheb was staying.

He had arrived ahead of us and the ceremonial welcome in his honour was already under way. Platters of food covered with handkerchiefs and wafting tempting smells were being brought in. Some people were being initiated into the Pir's fold with great fanfare and a *qawwali* had been arranged in their honour in the evening.

I was feeling ill at ease with the pomp and show of the place. It was something entirely new to me! At night when I joined the congregation, I was feeling very hungry. I told grandfather about it several times, but he just ignored it. I wanted to cry to express the state of my stomach, but could not.

I saw that people from among the audience were throwing currency notes at the singers to express their appreciation for the couplets they sang. Grandfather's hand went into his sherwani pocket again and again but then he would take it out empty from his pocket and curl up his nose to denote that he did not think much of couplet. I feared that if grandfather gave away the note to a singer, I would burst out crying and tell him that I was famished. Why should he give it away instead of feeding me? But things had not yet come to such a pass.

At last I fell asleep in the early hours of the morning, and when I woke up, I saw grandfather saying his prayers with other devotees. He had laid me to sleep in a comer. I woke up with a pang of hunger, but I told grandfather nothing about it.

Suddenly all the devotees stood and lined up in the passage. Pir Saheb was ready to depart and had stepped out into the verandah. His two associates were standing a little apart from him and the devotees were going to Pir Saheb, one by one, to receive his benediction. I saw that while shaking hands with him, they slipped a five-rupee or a ten-rupee note into his hand. Then they kissed his hand and stepped back, making room for the next devotee.

I looked at grandfather's face. I feared he would start crying, so overwhelmed he looked. And so humble, so helpless.

I was taking stock of the situation when I saw grandfather drawing near Pir Saheb. He quickly stepped forward and while shaking hands with him, slipped the two-rupee note into his palm.

He had bent low to kiss Pir Saheb's hand when the venerable man quickly withdrew it from grandfather's clasp and stretched it out towards another devotee. For a second grandfather stood stupefied. Then he caught hold of my arm and pulled me away.